The Fantastic Adventures of
Wee Dick

The Fantastic Adventures of Wee Dick

John H. Bruce

The Pentland Press Limited
Edinburgh • Cambridge • Durham • USA

First published in 1997 by
The Pentland Press Ltd.
1 Hutton Close
South Church
Bishop Auckland
Durham

British Library Cataloguing in Publication Data.
A catalogue record for this book is available
from the British Library.

ISBN 1 85821 456 4

Typeset by CBS, Felixstowe, Suffolk
Printed and bound by Antony Rowe Ltd., Chippenham

To Uncle John from Eleanor Anne

My Uncle John was a gifted story teller and I well remember as a child following him about the house demanding that he 'tell me a story'.

During his teaching career in Paisley generations of children were told stories about 'Wee Dick', a character, to whom I myself was never introduced.

For the last year of my Uncle's life he suffered from poor health and while dealing with all his business affairs I was amazed at the number of people who asked me if I knew what had happened to Wee Dick.

The final job was the clearance of a house which had been a family home for three generations with all that accumulates in that time. To my surprise and delight I discovered the rather tattered and dirty manuscript of 'Wee Dick'. It was unfinished, like all good serials, just waiting for the next adventure to begin. I have taken the liberty of finishing the story for those of you who remember Mr Bruce and Wee Dick and in memory of one who to many friends, neighbours and myself was simply Uncle John.

Eleanor A. Young

The Barrels

Once there was a boy called Dick. He was very small for his age and because he was the youngest of his family his mother always called him 'Wee Dick.' On the first day his mother took him to school the teacher looked down at him and said, 'So this is "Wee Dick".'

From that day on he was called Wee Dick by everyone, even his best friends, Bob and Harry.

Near where the boys lived was a wide river with factories along the banks. The school was not far from the river and the boys often took a short cut home to look at the old dockyard. It wasn't really a short cut but it was an interesting path with a hawthorn hedge on one side. It went to the top of a hill where there was a gate into a field that sloped down towards another hedge and beyond that the old dock. Here there was an old three masted sailing ship which was used as a training base for the Sea Cadets. Sometimes there would be a horse grazing in the field and the boys would stand on the gate and feed him bundles of grass.

One day, as they climbed onto the gate the boys noticed several large wooden barrels with black rusty iron hoops lying just inside the field, some were standing upright, others were lying on their sides, their insides looked clean and dry.

'There was a man once went over Niagara Falls in a

barrel,' said Harry. 'I wonder if it was one like that.'

'I read a story once about a man who rolled right round the world in a barrel,' Bob told them.

'That's a lot of rubbish,' laughed Harry. 'You couldn't roll round and round inside, you'd hurt yourself.'

Some of the other children from the school joined them and they all talked about the barrels. A boy called Jim had been to the circus and said that he had seen a clown going round the ring by making a barrel turn under his feet, and keeping his balance with two umbrellas. This gave them the idea to see if they could make a barrel roll like that but they were too heavy and they kept falling off.

Harry, who always liked to try new things, climbed into one of the barrels that was lying on its side. He pressed his feet and shoulders against the sides but the barrel would not move.

'Roll me around, roll me around!' he shouted.

The boys pushed the barrel, it was heavy but it wobbled unsteadily down the hill a short distance and came to a halt against a clump of thistles and long grass.

'What's it like then?' They all crowded round Harry as he crawled out.

'Nothing special' he answered. 'I think you'd soon get dizzy.'

'Let's have a shot,' said Bob.

The barrel was slowly pushed up the hill and Bob got himself into position.

'Push it hard,' he ordered and everyone pushed as hard as he could. The barrel rolled a little farther this time but it was again brought to a halt by a thick bunch of plants. They all took turns. Sometimes it went fairly well and sometimes it hardly moved at all.

3

Wee Dick was the last to try it. He got off to a good start and went quite far down the hill before the barrel veered off to the side and trundled to a standstill.

'That was great!' said Wee Dick. 'I want to do it again.'

'Weren't you dizzy?'

'Not much, I liked it. Come on, let's get back up the hill, I want another roll.'

Back up the hill they went and back into the barrel climbed Wee Dick.

'Push it hard this time,' he told them.

They shoved and back down the hill rolled the barrel only to veer off to the side and stop.

'That was hopeless,' moaned Dick. 'Give it a proper push next time.'

'You don't want to do it again,' moaned Bob.

'Yes, but much much faster,' answered Wee Dick, his dark eyes dancing with excitement.

Again the boys pushed the heavy barrel to the top of the hill.

'This is too much like hard work,' puffed Harry. 'I'm not doing it again.'

The barrel slowly began its third trip down the hill with Wee Dick inside. It gradually gathered speed and went well down the hill before veering to a stop.

'That was better,' cheered Wee Dick. 'Come on, let's have just one more try.'

Bob and Harry could not understand what their friend could find so great in this new activity and told him that they were going home and if he wanted to roll any more he could stay and do it himself.

The next morning at school Wee Dick told his pals that he could not wait till going home time to go barrel rolling again.

'You're daft,' was the general opinion of his classmates.

On the way home Wee Dick jumped and danced with impatience till they reached the field where the barrels were still lying on the grass. He was first over the fence and jumped into a barrel.

'Come on, give us a shove!' he shouted.

Bob and Harry stayed with Dick but the other boys turned away and walked on up the hill.

'Just one roll and that's the end,' said Bob firmly.

'Let's give it a real hard start,' Harry whispered to Bob. 'If we take a good run at it we can send it flying with our kicks.' Bob nodded and grinned. 'Are you ready Wee Dick?' they shouted as they walked well back from the barrel.

'Yes.'

'Well here goes.' They ran forward as fast as they could, raised their feet together and gave the barrel the hardest kick they could.

The heavy wooden thing with the iron hoops set off slowly down the hill but gradually gathered speed until it was bowling over and over, farther and farther away. Faster and faster it went towards the water. The two boys became alarmed.

'The dock!' yelled Harry. 'He'll crash through the hedge and into the dock!'

'Get out of the barrel, Dick! Get out of the barrel!' They raced after the barrel nearly falling in their frightened rush to try to stop it.

'Jump out, jump out!' they shouted, but nothing happened.

They were hardly more than an arm's length away from the runaway barrel when it crashed through the thin hedge and on to the dockside. They pushed through after it. The dockside was empty. There was no sign of Wee Dick or the barrel.

5

'He's gone into the water,' moaned Bob in despair. All Harry could do was to gaze around him open mouthed and say, 'Ohhhhhhhhhh!'

Slowly they tiptoed to the edge of the dock and looked down into the still oily water. Some old pieces of wood bobbed gently on the surface but they did not look like bits of a barrel. They half hoped, half dreaded to see Wee Dick struggling in the water. How quiet it was and how lonely. They felt frightened.

'He must have sunk straight away,' whispered Bob, in a voice that did not sound like his own.

'He didn't even make a splash,' said Harry, staring at the water in disbelief.

'We'll need to go and tell his mother.'

'I don't want to,' said Harry, tears filling his eyes.

'But we've got to,' said Bob and turned away.

They met no one as they slowly made their way out of the dock and along the road, each step bringing them nearer the street where they all lived.

When they reached the flats where Wee Dick lived they looked tearfully at each other and slowly began to climb the stairs.

They rang the bell and waited for the awful moment when Wee Dick's mother would open the door.

'Well, hello, boys.'

'It's Wee Dick,' was all that Harry could gasp.

'I'm sorry, you can't see him tonight,' answered his mother. 'He's in the bath. We're going out to his cousin's birthday party. Didn't he tell you? He came in just a few minutes ago absolutely filthy and I packed him straight off to the bathroom. Is it important or can it wait till tomorrow?'

'Oh yes, it can wait' Bob replied in a choked gasp.

The boys went back down the stairs and walked quietly to their own homes. They could hardly believe what had happened.

'Just wait till I see him tomorrow,' muttered Bob, 'What a mean trick to play!'

'But how did he get away so fast without us seeing him?' puzzled Harry. 'And what happened to the barrel?'

The next morning Bob and Harry waited for their friend.

'Why did you go off like that? You scared us? We thought you were drowned.'

'Oh no, I didn't drown,' said Wee Dick with a sly grin.

'We can see that,' said Bob getting cross. 'But how did you get away so fast? We were right behind you. Where did the barrel go? We didn't hear it splash into the water.'

Wee Dick however was very mysterious about it. He would not tell them how he had made his way home from the dockside and kept making silly remarks until the bell rang and they had to go into school.

At playtime Wee Dick ran away whenever his pals came near and at lunch time he hurried off home without them.

After school Harry and Bob grabbed Wee Dick by the arms and marched him up the hill to the field gate.

'Now you're going to show us how it's done,' insisted Bob.

'Great!' shouted Wee Dick. 'Let's roll the barrels.'

'No,' said Harry. 'It's too dangerous. You gave us a fright and I don't want another one.'

'It's not dangerous, just one roll,' insisted Dick.

'First tell us how you disappeared.'

'Not till you've given me a roll.'

The boys looked at each other. Reluctantly they watched Wee Dick climb into the barrel. They gave it a gentle push, it wobbled a little and came to a stop.

'Oh come on, a proper push, boys.'

This time they gave the barrel a harder push with their feet. As it gathered speed on its way downhill they followed close behind it. Just as the gathering speed began to alarm them a little the barrel crashed through the straggling hedge. Bob and Harry pushed through minutes behind it but it was gone and Wee Dick was nowhere to be seen. The oily water was still with some plastic bottles floating gently on the surface.

'The wee twister's done it again,' gasped Bob and angrily kicked a stone into the water. They watched the ripples spreading slowly to the side.

'Dick! Dick! Wee Dick where are you?' They called, but only heard a faint echo in reply.

On their way home they stopped at Wee Dick's house. His sister Ellen opened the door to their ring.

'Wee Dick says he's not coming out tonight. He'll see you tomorrow.'

So that was that.

The next morning when they tried to ask him, again he would not tell them what they wanted to know.

'All right then,' Harry warned him. 'If you're not going to tell us we're not going to be your pals any more.' He and Bob turned away.

Another boy, Edward came over.

'What's up with you lot?' he asked.

They told him but Edward would not believe that Wee Dick could have done anything particularly clever.

'You didn't watch him properly. He couldn't do that to me, I can tell you that.'

So Bob and Harry challenged Edward to come with them after school to see for himself. He came and as he watched the barrel bounding down the hill exclaimed, 'He'll kill himself!'

Down the hill and through the hedge went the barrel, hotly pursued by the three boys, but once it went through the hedge it just vanished. After Edward had organised a search the boys went back to Dick's house. He came to the door with a cheeky grin and said, 'I'm not coming out tonight. I'll see you at school tomorrow.'

Now Edward was a boy who did not let go easily. As the three of them left Wee Dick's flat, Bob and Harry asked if he could explain the mystery.

'It'll be something quite simple,' he answered frowning.

'What, for example?' demanded Harry impatiently.

'I don't know yet but I'll think about it.'

By morning, however, Edward had still not thought of anything.

'We'll get it out of him,' he promised. 'You'll see.'

But they did not. He kept dodging away from them whenever they came near in the playground. He came to school so late that he was nearly in trouble. He stayed behind to help the teacher tidy up and walked out of school and along the road with her, looking back at his pals with an impish grin.

'Teacher's pet,' they called after him.

Bob and Harry began to lose interest.

'Let him keep his silly secret,' they decided.

Edward was not so easily put off and decided to use tougher tactics.

He organised lots of unpleasant things. Boys would wait in doorways till Wee Dick passed then pounce on him, bumping him along the road, chanting, 'Tell us! Tell us!' with each bump.

In a corner of the playground was a tap that the janitor used when he cleaned the windows or hosed the playground. It was turned on using a special key but some of the boys found a way to turn it on without the key. Wee Dick had his head put under the tap. In spite of it all however, he kept dodging every question about barrels. Luckily Dick was a popular boy so none of these pranks was carried too far.

By now most of the children had heard of the mysterious vanishing trick. Edward had boasted that he would get it out of him somehow and was beginning to lose his patience. He finally lost his temper and began twisting Wee Dick's arm behind his back. Dick screamed just as the headmaster came into the playground. Edward, a tall sturdy boy looked so much bigger than Wee Dick that he was taken into the headmaster's office and as a punishment for bullying was suspended from the school football team for a month. There was to be an important game that week, Edward was the star player. The whole class turned against Wee Dick. They told him that he was to blame for Edward's suspension and that nobody would speak to him again until he told them what they wanted to know.

'And what's more,' added Annie Downie. 'You're not coming to my party next month.' Annie Downie's parties were famous. There was always so much to eat, lots and lots of ice cream and super prizes for the games. This was indeed punishment.

After one very lonely day at school Wee Dick agreed to tell them. A crowd gathered round.

'It's sort of difficult to explain,' he began.

'Tell us, tell us,' chanted the children.

'You see, it's like this. You'll never understand.'

'He's trying to trick us again,' grunted Edward turning away. The others began to do the same. Wee Dick called after them, 'Wait, wait, come with me to the field and I'll show you.'

It was late autumn and the evening was cold and beginning to get foggy. In spite of that quite a crowd of children followed Edward, Bob, Harry and Wee Dick up the hill to the barrels. Edward was the organiser.

'Now this time we're not going to run after the barrel. We're going down the hill and through the hedge first and then we'll see just what happens when it comes through. I'll give a whistle when we're ready. Give the barrel a good push to start it off properly.'

The three boys set off down the hill. Edward gave the orders. He sent Bob along the hedge at one side and Harry at the other while he himself took the middle position. A few minutes later he put his fingers in his mouth and whistled.

Six or seven boys stood well back then ran forward and sent the barrel rolling with great kicks. It set off like an express train. It rolled and bounded as it gathered speed. There was a half buried boulder in its track and as it hit it the barrel seemed to take off. It soared above the grass and Edward had to duck as it flew over the hedge, sailed right over his head and landed with a tremendous splash in the water below him.

The boys ran to the edge of the dock and peered over in dismay. The other children came pushing through the hedge shouting, 'Where is he? Where is he?'

The barrel was floating upright, bobbing and turning gently. Wee Dick's dark curly head could only just be seen between his hands holding on to the edge of the barrel. They could hear him crying.

'Help! Help! Help!'

They all seemed rooted to the spot and could only stare.

It was Bob who first noticed that the barrel was floating slowly but steadily towards the entrance of the dock and the river beyond.

'You're going into the river!' he shouted.

They ran along the edge of the dock following the barrel on its trip out into the river. There were some slimy steps going down to the water's edge where there was a life belt hanging on a wooden post.

'We'll throw you the life belt. Grab it,' they shouted.

Edward was hoised up to lift the life belt off its hook. It was heavier than he had expected and in his excitement his aim was poor. It landed nowhere near the barrel which was now bobbing steadily down stream.

The boys stood together and looked down at Wee Dick who stared up at them helplessly as the current caught the barrel and swept it out into the river. It grew smaller and smaller.

'Look!' shouted Harry, pointing upstream.

They all turned. Out of the evening mist loomed a large vessel on her way down to the sea. Slowly she grew bigger and bigger. The high prow, the towering mast, the bridge, then they could hear the steady thudding churning sound of her propellers.

She sounded a deep blast of warning on her hooter as she turned the bend in the river and began to disappear into the mist. The boys watched as the backwash splashed up against the dock walls. There was now no sign of the barrel or of Wee Dick. Now they would have to go and tell somebody what had happened. This time Bob and Harry knew that when they went to Wee Dick's house he would not have got home before them.

The Journey Begins

As the *Merchant Enterprise* moved slowly down the river, seaman Miller, known to all his mates as Dusty, was at the stern. One of the heavy mooring ropes had caught on some floating timber and was dragging it along behind as the ship got under way. Dusty, leaning over the side trying to free the rope, noticed a barrel floating quite close to the side of the ship. Suddenly he saw the frightened white face of a small boy looking up at him, his small hands clutching desperately on to the side of the barrel.

'Come over here quickly!' Dusty yelled to his mates, then without waiting he climbed over the side and hand over hand slid down the rope towards the foaming water. Holding the rope with his legs and one arm Dusty bent forward and grabbing Wee Dick hauled him out of the barrel. He swung him round and held him close to his chest. The sailors on deck hauled the rope, raising them slowly upwards. The timber came free and crashed against the side of the ship just as the barrel was drawn under the stern by the propellers and splintered like a matchbox. Wee Dick and Dusty landed safely on the deck.

Wee Dick was unconscious as he was carried below to be examined by the ship's doctor. He was dried, wrapped in warm blankets and put to bed in a spare cabin to recover from concussion and the shock. The ship was gathering speed out into the open sea when the captain got the message about his unexpected passenger. A message was radioed ashore. Wee Dick was safe.

He slept soundly till the next morning and felt much better although the doctor insisted that he stay in bed for another day.

'Are you feeling better now?' asked Dusty when he took in some toast.

Wee Dick nodded. He could not remember everything that had happened to him. He sat up in the bunk and at once felt dizzy.

The next day the doctor said that he could get up for a little while and get some fresh air. His clothes had all been cleaned and once he had dressed he went up on deck. There was a stiff breeze blowing and the ship was well out in a choppy sea. It was not long before he began to feel seasick and had to go back to the cabin again.

'You'll feel better once you've eaten,' reassured Dusty, and firmly took him by the arm and led him to the crew's dining room.

The *Merchant Enterprise* was a cargo vessel and the sailors being unused to company made a great fuss over their small passenger.

Wee Dick had little appetite for the large plate of bacon and eggs that was put down before him, but did manage to eat a little bread and soup and have a cup of tea. Dusty was right. He did feel better after that and spent the afternoon on deck watching the waves and exploring his new surroundings. He decided that from now on he was going to enjoy himself.

'So, my lad,' said one of the sailors whom everyone called

Nobby, 'you are coming the whole trip with us. There and back.'

Dusty explained that the ship would not be putting into land for several days because she was behind time and had to make the port by a set date or the shipping company would lose a lot of money. Wee Dick would have to stay with them until they made the return trip.

The crew gave Dick the run of the ship. As he was an inquisitive boy he asked lots of questions. The sailors liked him and enjoyed talking to him so it was not long before he had learned all their names and what their jobs were on the ship.

Days passed and the weather grew steadily warmer. One day as Wee Dick looked out over the ship's rail he saw flying fish skimming over the water. It was exciting. They didn't just jump, they really flew more like a flock of shiny birds.

Dusty told him that the next day the sailors would all change into shorts and light clothes since they were now in tropical seas.

'What about me?' asked Wee Dick.

'Oh you'll be all right too, Nobby's made you some tropical outfits out of some old sheets. You're a lucky boy, Nobby's clever that way.'

The next morning when Dick woke up he found new white shorts and shirts beside his bunk. Yes, he decided, he was indeed a lucky boy to be on this trip, with a cabin to himself and all the crew looking after him so well. Dick decided that day that he was going to be a sailor when he grew up.

It was Nobby who told him that he should learn to tie all the knots that sailors use. With a length of string he showed him what to do. He gave Dick a board with holes in it and told him to practise the knots until he could tie them behind his

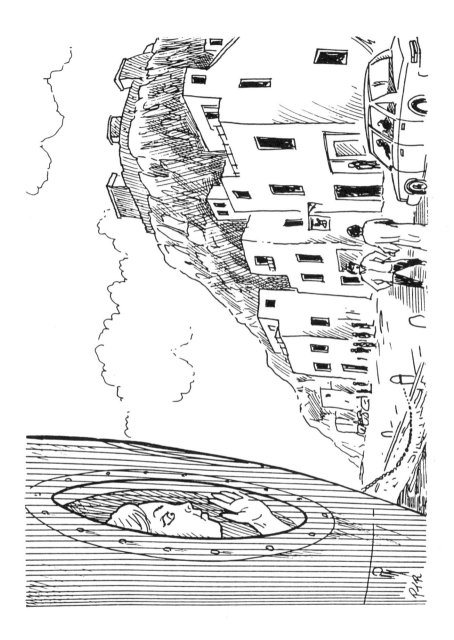

17

back and with his eyes closed.

One morning when he awoke, Wee Dick had the feeling that there was something different. The movement seemed to have stopped, as had the steady throb of the engines. He was sure that he could hear motor cars. He crawled along to the end of his bunk and looked out of the porthole.

They had reached port. Outside the early morning sun was shining in a bright blue sky. Tall thin white buildings rose up like steps throwing purple shadows on to each other. Behind the buildings rose a towering rock and he could just make out the shape of a castle-like building on the top. By pressing his face hard against the glass he was able to look down and see that the *Merchant Enterprise* was tied up at a quay. Already cars and lorries were moving alongside and tall cranes were swinging the cargo ashore. Wee Dick was so excited that he didn't wash, but pulling on his clothes as he went, rushed up on deck.

Dusty told him that this was to be a very short call and as everybody would be busy he was to keep out of the way.

There was so much to watch he did not go below deck for food but watched the traffic below and the women, carrying huge baskets of fruit on their heads, walking along the quayside. Wee Dick had never seen people carry such huge loads on their heads before.

By afternoon the cargo was all unloaded and Dusty said that there would be some time to wait before high tide. He suggested that they could climb to the Crusader's castle on the top of the rock.

They set off just after one, Dusty carrying a big net bag over his shoulder. As soon as they stepped off the gang plank the women and girls with the fruit baskets crowded round them. Dusty was ready and soon had four fat melons, some

18

oranges and bananas in his net bag.

They set off together through the narrow streets of the town, grateful to walk in the shade of the buildings to keep out of the scorching heat of the afternoon sun. The shops had no windows but were open onto the street where the shopkeepers sat on the pavement, surrounded by their goods, calling out to attract customers as they passed by.

As they went on past these stalls the streets gradually became steeper and changed into broad shallow steps. It was a busy thoroughfare. Women and girls with enormous bundles and baskets balanced precariously on their heads walked gracefully past. Donkeys with loads piled high on their backs, pulled along by young bare footed boys, even men on bicycles jostled and pushed their way up and down the winding pathway. Suddenly the buildings stopped and they were out in the open. The hot sun shone fiercely down as they followed the path which wound round along the very edge of the steep rock.

Wee Dick could see the harbour and the *Merchant Enterprise* looking quite small tied up at the quay. An American naval ship was anchored out in the bay, the sun reflecting on its silver hull like a mirror, and a white and gold cruising liner was tied up at another berth.

The path followed the rock face. Sometimes when he looked up Dick could see the walls of the Crusader's castle quite close above him and then it would seem to disappear as the path carried on round the other side of the hill. He had never known that the sun could be so hot. He was glad when Dusty suggested that they stop in a shady spot and have some of the fruit. He cut a large slice of red water melon. The melon was sweet and juicy, Dick had to lean forward to stop the juice from running down his clothes. He had never tasted water melon before but it was delicious. He could have sat there for longer but Dusty said that they didn't have time, so back out into the hot sun they went to continue the climb to the castle. Suddenly a little monkey scampered across the path, a tiny baby clinging to its underside.

'Look Dusty, a monkey!' shouted Dick excitedly.

'Have you never seen monkeys in the zoo?'

'Yes, but that is a real one. It's free with its baby. Look, there's another one!'

They passed more monkeys as they got nearer the castle. The castle seemed to grow out of the rock itself. Trees and bushes sprouted from great cracks in the walls. It seemed more like a walled town than just a castle. Crowds of other people had reached the top before them. There was a group of American sailors laughing and joking together and some tourists from the liner. Many of them had ridden up on donkeys, which were patiently standing in the shade of the walls waiting to take them back down. Round the walls were stalls selling all kinds of souvenirs, postcards and straw hats. A little way apart from them all sat a dark skinned man with a hood over his head. He didn't seem to be selling anything. A sailor was sitting on a small stool in front of him and the man was holding his hand.

'Is he telling the sailor's fortune?' Wee Dick asked Dusty, in a whisper.

'Yes, that's what he's doing.'

'We had a fortune teller at our school fair but it was just one of the teachers dressed up. Is he dressed up too?'

'Not this one. He's a real fortune teller. He's quite famous.'

'Has he ever told your fortune when you were here before?'

'Yes.'

'What did he tell you? Was it good? Did it come true?'

20

'I can't remember what he told me,' answered Dusty. 'He said that I would forget it if I took a drink from his brass cup but it was my own choice whether to drink or not. He said that I would remember it again just before it came true and that that was the best way. I drank out of his cup. Perhaps I didn't like what he told me.'

'I don't see any brass cup.' Wee Dick watched the sailor carefully until he got up and went over to join his mates.

'*He* didn't drink anything. Dusty, are you making fun of me?'

'Oh no, not at all,' answered Dusty. 'Do you want him to tell your fortune?'

'Yes, yes, but I'm not going to drink anything. I'm going to remember it and see if it comes true.'

Dusty led him over to the man and said something to him that Wee Dick could not quite catch. The man threw the hood back from his face and looked at him with piercing dark eyes. Dusty held out some money but the man shook his head and said a few words.

'He wants you to give him something of your own,' said Dusty.

Wee Dick had nothing but his clothes. He looked about him.

'But I haven't got anything,' he said.

The man spoke again.

'You're to give him what you have in your pocket,' replied Dusty.

Not long after he had arrived on board the *Merchant Enterprise* one of the sailors had carved a small wooden barrel as a souvenir for Wee Dick. He pushed his hands deep into the pocket of his shorts and his fingers closed round the barrel. He didn't want to part with it. It was beautifully carved, and carefully hollowed out inside. It had 'Dick' neatly carved round the hoops. The sailor who had carved it had said, 'Now that's a lucky charm for you. Keep it with you all the time.'

In his other pocket he felt the piece of rope that he used for practising his knots. Dick took the barrel and the rope out of his pockets and held them out towards the man with the dark eyes.

The fortune teller took them in his hands and looked at them closely turning them over and over. Then he handed back the little barrel and taking the rope in his hands, began to weave it into a strange looking pattern with four loose ends sticking out at the corners.

He spoke in clear English but with a strange accent, 'Your fortune is here in this knot. If you want to know what it is you must pull the rope free.'

He handed the knotted rope back to Dick and pulled his hood back over his head. As Dusty and Wee Dick turned to leave Dusty asked, 'Well then, are you going to pull it loose?'

'No, not just now. I want to climb right up to the battlements.'

It was no wonder that the Crusaders had built their fortress on this great high rock. No enemy could have crept up on them unawares. The sea stretched out all around them for miles and any enemy who had managed to land would still have had to climb the towering rock. The view was tremendous but it was getting late. They had to return to the ship. Halfway down the hill Dusty sat on a rock in the shade to eat some more fruit.

'We'll eat some of this now,' he said taking another small melon. 'Then I can get some more before we go back on ship.'

Just as they were finishing eating Wee Dick suddenly said, 'Shush.'

'I don't hear anything,' mumbled Dusty through a mouthful of melon.

'Listen. There it is again, something's crying. Over there behind those rocks.'

There was indeed a faint whimpering sound, as if someone or something was in pain. Very cautiously they crept up and peered over the rocks.

Crouched below, huddled in a corner was a small monkey, not a baby, but not quite fully grown. Its right forepaw had a deep cut in it which had stopped bleeding, but flies were swarming round it and the little animal was trying vainly to wave them away with its other paw.

'Oh the poor thing,' whispered Dick. 'Can't we do something to help it?'

'We can try but I doubt if we can do much good,' answered Dusty, as he stretched towards the little monkey, which shrank back from him against the rock. Dusty made soothing noises and picked up the little animal. He took a handkerchief from his pocket and tied it round the little animal's paw. 'I don't know what we can do with the beastie now,' he said. Dick jumped excitedly on the spot.

'Give him to me,' he said. 'Let me keep it. I'll look after it.'

He carried the monkey close to him, back down the rock through the streets and along the quay. While Dusty went off bargaining for more fruit Dick went straight on board and down to his cabin.

Shortly afterwards the *Merchant Enterprise* slowly moved away from the quayside into the bay past the cruise ship and the American battleship out to the ocean again. Wee Dick went off to find the ship's doctor. He was attending to a sailor who had hurt his arm but promised to come to see the monkey as soon as he was free. Wee Dick returned to his cabin where he washed the monkey's little paw and made a nest for it at the end of his bunk.

It did look very sick.

The doctor, when he came in, shook his head. He said that he didn't think the monkey would live but he dressed the wound properly.

Wee Dick gently stroked the little animal's head and fed it titbits of melon and banana.

The ship sailed on through the night.

Later Dick went on deck and watched the stars reflected in the dark deep water. Dusty came over and leaned on the rail beside him.

'Have you pulled the ends of your fortune knot yet?' he asked. 'You could pull the ends and see if your monkey is going to live.'

Dick shook his head, he would not show the knot to anyone, not even his special pals.

'I don't need to,' he answered. 'It is going to live, I don't need to worry.'

The monkey did live, although when Dick looked at it the next morning it was so weak it could hardly lift its head. Dick sat beside it all day feeding it tiny pieces of fruit and sips of water. That night the doctor looked in on his new patient and said that he thought he might just pull through after all.

Its recovery was slow and the paw never completely healed but he was able to hop around quite happily on three legs and it was not very long before he would sit on Dick's shoulder watching all that was going on around him.

He would follow Dick everywhere and as he grew stronger, became mischievous, knocking things over and pulling clothes

out of the drawers in the cabin, scattering them all over the floor.

The sailors kept asking Dick what he was going to call the monkey and suggested all sorts of names but none of them seemed quite right. Because of the damaged paw the monkey always walked rather jerkily on three legs holding the weak paw close to him for protection.

One day, as he came hopping after Dick on the deck, one of the sailors called out, 'Hey Dick. There's your monkey bobbin' along after you.'

Dick at once decided what he was going to call his pet and so the monkey was called Bobbin. The sailors all laughed and said, 'That's not a proper name for a monkey.'

But Bobbin it was and Bobbin it stayed.

Bobbin soon learned to untie knots with his sharp little teeth and would annoy Dick when he was practising his knots by pulling at the ends.

One day as Dusty was watching them he said, 'Why don't you give Bobbin your fortune knot and see if he can pull it loose if you haven't managed it yourself yet?'

Wee Dick told him that he had not tried to pull it out and Bobbin was not going to be allowed to try either.

'Are you scared to try it?' asked Dusty.

'Well I'm not sure. But anyway, you must have been a bit scared of your fortune if you drank out of that little brass cup,' Dick replied with a little smile.

'Maybe you're right there,' answered Dusty and he never mentioned the knot again.

Over the next few days the weather became hotter, damp and clammy. A haze hid the horizon and even the sun seemed to be a large blurry glow in the sky.

One afternoon a sailor pointed into the distance where a

range of mountains with sharp peaks was appearing gradually through the haze.

'We'll dock there tomorrow morning,' he said. 'This is our main port of call. We will be here for a while unloading the cargo and there is to be a repair done to one of the engines.'

Dusty told Dick, 'Look, you'll be on your own a lot while we're here. There is a lot of work to be done but I'll show you around a bit and then you can go on shore on your own if you want. The people here are all very friendly so you should get on all right.'

When Wee Dick got up the next morning the ship was slowly moving towards her berth. Although it was very early the day was already hot and steamy and his shirt was sticking to his skin. From the deck he could see a large town. The houses had flat roofs and the streets were lined with palm trees. Behind the town the mountains seemed to tower into the sky. The streets seemed to be very busy with cars, bicycles, donkeys pulling little carts or with huge bundles on their backs. And camels – lots of camels.

Just then someone tapped him on the shoulder.

'Come on now, it's time for breakfast.'

He turned and went below.

Dick and the Crocodile

The next few days were just as the sailors had said. They had little time to spare for Wee Dick, being busy unloading the cargo. In the muggy heat they were tired when they were off duty and when they went on shore they did not always want a small boy with them. During the days, however, Dick went on shore alone and explored the quayside.

Early every morning women, girls and sometimes young boys would come to the quayside to sell fresh fruit from baskets. The sailors often gave Dick a little pocket money and he was able to buy what he wanted. There seemed to be great competition among the fruit sellers and often the young boys were chased away by the older women.

They were smiling, friendly people with golden tanned skin, dark hair and very clear blue eyes. That was the first thing that Dick noticed, the blue, blue eyes. There was another group of people that seemed to keep separate from the crowds in little groups of their own. They had dark brown eyes and both the men and women had long blonde hair which they tied back with strips of brightly coloured cloth. It did not take Dick long to notice that these two groups of people kept well apart and were never seen talking to each other. He asked Dusty about it one evening.

'Why do the dark haired people never speak to the fair

haired ones here?'

'I don't know,' answered Dusty, 'but it seems to have always been like that. Maybe it's because of something that happened long ago. If you try to talk about it they turn and walk away and say nothing. Ask Simon, he knows a lot about history.'

Dick noticed that every day there was one particular small boy who came to the quayside. He was about his own age, he seldom had much fruit and he was often chased away by the women. He stood on the edge of the crowd as if he did not really expect anyone to buy from him. Dick watched him and decided he was going to buy his fruit from this boy.

He dodged round behind the crowd of women towards the boy and held out his money. The child smiled broadly and held out his hand. Just then one of the women pushed forward and tried to take the money. Dick held it tightly and shook his head, he turned back to the boy and that was how he met Tinka.

They became friends and met every day, even when there was no fruit to sell. Each day Dick went farther and farther along the quayside and now that he was no longer alone he would follow his new friend down the little streets that led off the waterfront. There were a few modern buildings but none of them was very high. There was a railway station with sidings and huge engines that pulled coaches and trucks along narrow tracks. The engines were all old fashioned steam engines with funnels that hissed and spluttered as they pulled in and out of the station. There were a few motor cars in the town, but these always seemed to be broken down with steam coming from the engines or their bonnets up and several men all looking into the engine and arguing about what should be done.

'It's the heat,' Dusty told him. 'Out here the camels and the donkeys are far more reliable. They're used to the heat.'

Dick never found out where Tinka lived. Tinka knew a few words of English, enough to be able to sell his fruit and some that he had picked up from sailors in port. Wee Dick tried to teach him more English and was able to pick up a little of Tinka's strange language so they got along very well. Dusty told him that Tinka might not have a real home or even any family. Things like that happened often in some parts of the world.

Sometimes when they were out together Dick took Bobbin with him. He had a little chain fixed to a belt round the monkey's waist and the other end fastened to a watch strap round his wrist. Bobbin was inclined to scamper off and could sometimes be a nuisance. Once when he had scampered off he knocked over a tin of paint and one of the sailors had threatened to throw him to the sharks.

One day Nobby was off duty and asked Dick if he would like to come with him across the desert to see the ruined temple where there was a giant crocodile as old as the world.

'How do they know it's that old?' asked Dick.

'Well it's what they say here. Anyway the last time I saw it, it looked old enough.'

'How do we cross the desert. Is it a real one?'

'It's a little one. Maybe it's not a real desert but it's sandy enough for us. We'll go on camels.'

With Bobbin on his chain perched on his shoulder Dick set off with Nobby through the narrow streets until they had passed all the houses. One moment they were walking through shady alleys and the next they were standing with the houses behind them with a sandy stony plain stretching ahead of them into the distance. A crowd had gathered there. The

31

camel drivers shouted and argued loudly while arrangements were made for hire. Nobby bargained with two drivers and then led the way over to where a row of camels sat patiently waiting.

'Up you go then, you and your monkey,' said Nobby as he helped Dick climb onto the animal's back and then got on to the next camel himself. Wee Dick clung on tightly as the camel rose, hind legs first. He felt as if he was a great height off the ground and the camel's unsteady gait made him feel unsure that he would not fall off. At first he held on tightly not looking at anything but after a few moments he began to get used to the unusual movement, relaxed and enjoyed himself.

It certainly didn't seem to be a quick method of travel but when he looked back the town was already disappearing into the haze.

There was nothing much to see except rocks and sand but he did hear the sound of a train over to his right and he could faintly make out an engine pulling a line of trucks.

'Couldn't we have gone by train?' he asked.

'It doesn't go to the temple. It's for the quarry, besides I thought a camel ride would be much more exciting,' replied Nobby.

Just as Dick was beginning to get a bit drowsy from watching nothing but sand and stones Nobby whistled and pointed ahead. The temple was appearing through the haze. He could see the outline of broken walls, pillars and clumps of palm trees. The procession of camels stopped in the shade of one of the walls. The beasts knelt and the riders dismounted. Dick felt his legs a bit unsteady as he took his first steps back on the ground.

They walked through a gap in the walls and ahead of them

was the temple

The buildings were in ruins. Several pillars had fallen and were lying broken on the ground. Facing them were eight gigantic stone statues but they were all damaged. Every one of them had lost its face which seemed strange, almost as if it had been done deliberately, because the bodies were still clearly and sharply carved and the feet were not worn by the weather at all. Beneath the statues were panels of stone with writing carved into them in strangely shaped letters.

Wee Dick was just about to ask why the statues had no faces as they moved on through an archway and his attention was caught by a large pool of green scummy water.

It was about the size of a swimming pool but no one could want to swim in that water. A crowd had gathered on one side and it was clear that they were all waiting for something to happen.

'I don't see any crocodile.'

'Just you wait a minute,' said Nobby with a wise nod.

From behind a ruined wall came two men, one was carrying a large basket on his head and the other had a kind of long handled pitch fork. When the basket was laid down at the poolside Wee Dick could see that it held the remains of a goat that had been roughly hacked up without being skinned. The basket was buzzing with swarming flies and the smell made him feel sick. He turned away.

The man with the pitchfork stuck it into the basket to lift out a piece of the meat which he lifted high and flung into the pool with a great shout. The splash sent up a shower of green water which splattered Dick, leaving ugly green spots on his white T-shirt. A second piece of meat was thrown into the pool and as it sank into the water Nobby pointed. A V-shaped ripple was spreading down the water and Dick could see that at the head of this was a huge snout and two glittering eyes. The man with the fork threw a third piece of meat. The huge mouth opened, showing long yellow fangs. The crocodile made a leap into the air to catch the meat before it landed in the water. Its tail must have helped it because it struck the water with a tremendous splash. This was indeed a huge animal and very ugly, far uglier than any photograph Wee Dick had ever seen in any book.

All this time Bobbin had been sitting quietly on Dick's shoulder. Now, while he had been on the camel journey, the watch strap had become tight and uncomfortable so Dick had loosened it and had been holding the chain in his hand but as he had been watching the crocodile he had released his hold.

The splash startled Bobbin. He leaped down and in seconds had scampered off and disappeared among the feet of the crowd. Wee Dick ran after and tried to stamp his foot on the end of the trailing chain but in his rush he did not notice how close he was to the edge of the pool.

There was a narrow stone path round the edge of the pool, it was uneven with large gaps where stone had broken away. Bobbin turned at the top of the pool and scampered along this path with Dick in pursuit. As he stamped his foot down on the end of the chain the loose stones gave way beneath him and before he could stop himself he fell forwards into the dark dirty water.

As he surfaced he saw the great evil looking snout turn towards him. He struggled. The edge of the pool was too high and he could not get a grip of anything on the sides. Then he saw an opening in the stonework. There was a small shallow arch in the poolside. He thought he could hide there. Without stopping to think he flung himself into the opening and pulled himself out of the water.

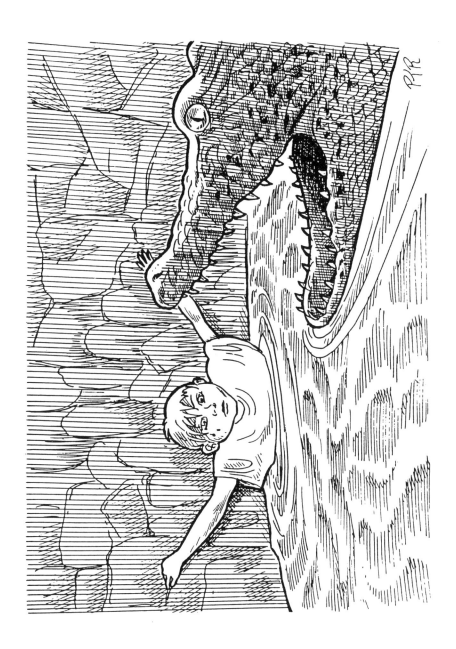

He kept on his hands and knees and crawled deep back into the hole as fast as he could until he was exhausted and lay panting on the floor. After a few moments when he got his breath back he looked around him to see that he was in some sort of tunnel. It was quiet. No sound of the beast coming after him. When he looked back he could see a small slit of light at the opening of the tunnel, but nothing would make him go back there where that crocodile might be waiting for him.

He crawled on into the darkness until he realised that the roof was no longer just above his head. He stood up carefully and stretched his arms above him slowly. He could not touch the roof. It was dark and he could see nothing. He moved very cautiously along, his arms outstretched feeling ahead of him as he went. He could sense that he was gradually moving upwards and then ahead of him he saw a faint light. As he moved slowly closer to the light he realised that it was shining down a shaft like a well. He could look up and see the sky but although he shouted and shouted no one came to look down. There was however enough light for him to see his surroundings. The tunnel ended here, but in front of him was a flight of stone steps going up into darkness. There was nothing else to do. He slowly climbed the stairs, counting as he went.

Nineteen, twenty. They stopped. Ahead of him was a stone wall, he could go no farther. He felt the wall with his hands but there was no opening. He would have to go back down.

He was just about to turn when there was a low rumbling sound. He felt a movement in the step beneath him. The wall slid open ahead of him. His eyes were dazzled by light.

This was his way out!

He stepped forward and looked around him, but before he could take anything in, there was a dull thud behind him. The stone wall swung back into place so neatly that, if he had not just walked through it he would never have believed that there had been an opening there at all. He pressed on the stones with his fingers and banged on the wall with his fists. He stamped on the floor to try to make the wall move, but it remained solid.

He was in a long narrow hall with two rows of thick pillars all the way down. At the other end was a huge statue of a man seated on a throne. The statue seemed to be wearing a long robe that left its chest bare but hid its legs under folds of cloth. The feet showed out below and had long pointed toe nails like the sharp claws of a wild animal. The thing that scared him most however was that the statue, which was so carefully carved, did not seem to have any face.

At the foot of the throne was a long narrow opening in the floor from which came a flickering blue light that lit the hall brilliantly one moment then seemed to die away. When the light was at its strongest and the hall brightly lit, the head of the statue was round and smooth, like an egg. As the light dimmed however Dick was able to make out a face which seemed to be watching him from deep set eyes. They seemed to peer right through him and made him feel afraid.

Was it only a trick of the light and the shadows?

Wee Dick was scared but he was also curious. He moved slowly towards the opening in the floor and peered down. The light came from so far down that he could not see where it came from. As he looked his eyes started to sting from the bluish haze that was rising from the slot in the floor with the light. He took a step back and as he did so looked straight up at the face.

Close to, this was not as smooth as an egg, but had lines and wrinkles all over. They did not make features but caught the flickering light and made shadows.

Dick began to feel less afraid. He decided that he must be in some kind of temple. Nobody would build a temple unless they could visit it. So how did they get in and out? It could not be by the way he had come so there must be another door. He began to walk round the hall to search for the entrance but could see no signs of one anywhere. Behind the pillars the light was poor so he ran his hands over the walls as he went but the stonework was smooth to the touch. Now and then he stamped his feet to test the floor but he could find nothing.

As he went behind the statue he saw a square opening in the wall just about the height of his shoulders. A long shaft sloped up into the darkness. He shouted up it and heard his own voice echo in the distance. He wondered if he should try to climb up this sloping tunnel. It must go somewhere. He would have another look for a door and if there was nothing else he would try that.

He turned away but just then there came a booming sound from the tunnel. It was a voice, someone was calling.

'Wee Dick. Wee Dick. Are you there?'

'Yes! Yes, I'm down here.' He shouted as loud as he could up the shaft.

He recognised Nobby's voice.

'Wait there for Bobbin. He's coming down.'

He waited peering up into the darkness until he heard a scuttling sound and the little monkey appeared out of the opening with a rope tied round his middle and a stone tied to the end of the rope which stretched back up into the darkness.

38

'Have you got it?'

'Yes.'

'Tie the rope round your waist. Take the stone off and shout when you are ready. Hold tight and I'll pull you out.'

Slowly he was pulled up the dark tunnel.

He blinked as he came out into the daylight again. When he was pulled clear he found that he was not inside the ruined walls any longer.

They were on a rocky slope not far from some bare stone hills. Here and there some desert plants were blowing in the dusty breeze. He had been pulled through a low archway rather like the one at the pool. Quite a crowd had gathered.

They were standing inside the broken walls of what looked like a stone tank through which a thin stream of water was trickling slowly downhill.

'You gave us all some fright! Lucky for you some folk knew about this old cistern here,' said Nobby, waving his arm towards the stone walls.

'When we saw you go into the tunnel we couldn't think how to get you out again until one of the camel drivers told me that in the rainy season the stream here floods into the crocodile pool and cleans it out, so up we came, Bobbin and all. He's your lucky mascot all right.'

At that moment Wee Dick was too pleased to be back with Nobby to tell him that there was more than a water channel. He could tell him afterwards.

They set off back down the rocky slope to the ruined temple and the camels. Then it was back to the town and the quayside. His clothes were filthy from his fall into the pool so he was glad to get back to the *Merchant Enterprise*, have a shower and put on some clean things.

It was a fine story for Nobby to tell all his mates at mealtime that evening.

'Wee Dick there has the devil's own luck,' said Dusty, and they all agreed.

Inside the Temple

The next morning all the sailors were busy and no one had time to spare to listen to Wee Dick's story. He tried to tell Tinka about his adventure but this was difficult with the little English that the boy knew. Dick tried drawing pictures of himself on a camel, of the temple and of the crocodile but the next part of the story he could just not make him understand. It was only when he drew a picture of the statue with a faceless head that Tinka seemed to know what he was talking about. He shrank back, shaking his head and turned and ran away. He didn't listen to Wee Dick's calls for him to come back again. This was another puzzle for Wee Dick.

The next day it was even hotter and work on the ship and along the waterfront stopped. Dick was sitting beside Nobby outside a small café built in the shade of a clump of palm trees.

'Nobby, you know that tunnel I was in? It doesn't just go down to the crocodile pool.'

'Doesn't it then? Where does it go?'

Wee Dick told him but he could see to his annoyance that Nobby did not believe him.

'You don't believe me,' he shouted crossly.

'Well, if you saw what you say you saw, why has no one else discovered it before now? You were a bit shaken and dazed when we pulled you out of the shaft. Do you know what is meant by a hallucination?'

'Yes,' answered Dick sulkily. 'It means you are seeing things that are not really there. But I did see it. I did! I did! I did!'

Nobby did not go on with the argument. It was too hot. Wee Dick hunched up looking cross and moody.

'What's up with our wee barrel boy then?' asked Simon as he came over and sat down beside them.

'Tell him, Dick.'

'No, he'll just say I'm making it up too.'

'How can I say that until I know what it is you are going to say?'

So Dick told it all over again and Simon listened in silence.

'Well,' he said thoughtfully, 'it is certainly what you might call a tall tale. Nobby is right when he says that hot countries can play tricks on people who are not used to them. The heat dries you up and you lose salt and there are all sorts of bugs that you don't get at home. You did get quite a shock with that crocodile but if you like we could go around a bit and ask. The man to ask is the dock foreman. He can speak a good bit of English and he's been here all his life. We'll see him tomorrow.'

The next morning Dick waited impatiently for Simon to speak to the dock foreman. He was a big strong looking man with piercing blue eyes and a laugh that showed all his teeth. Like all the people in the town he was very friendly. At the midday break Wee Dick tugged at Simon's arm and said, 'Simon, you were going to talk to the foreman.'

The man came aboard and they all sat down to listen to Dick's tale. When he had finished Simon turned to the foreman and said, 'Well then, what do you make of all that?'

The foreman did not say anything for a minute or two and then not looking at either of them but staring off into the distance said, 'In the wet weather you can see the stream pouring down into the channel and you can watch the water pouring into the pool. It rains so heavily sometimes that the pool often overflows. Sometimes the crocodile swims out with the flood and has to be chased back. When I was a boy I went with two friends. To show how brave we were, we crawled from the cistern down into the crocodile pool. The water was very low at the time and the crocodile was sunning itself on the sloping edge of the pool. Once we had proved how brave we were we crawled back up the channel again and went home. It's very dark in there.'

Having said this the foreman got up and walked down the gangway to the dockside without looking at either Simon or Dick again.

'Well then,' said Simon shaking his head, 'his story and yours don't quite agree, do they?'

Wee Dick couldn't understand it. He knew he had not been dreaming. Maybe there was another channel that he had not seen. The more he thought about it the more he felt that there was something that he was not being told.

The foreman had not said that the pillared hall and the statue did not exist. He had told a story about the water channel to make him think that that was all there was to know about. Wee Dick was not satisfied at all.

He decided that there was only one thing he could do. He had to go back to the ruined temple and find his way back to the hall. Now that he knew how to get there and back out again he had nothing to fear. Of course he would have to have someone with him as a witness. He would never manage to persuade any of the sailors to come with him so that left only

Tinka. Now again, Tinka had been frightened away by a drawing of the statue without the face. Why was that? He would have to find out.

Several days passed and the little fruit seller did not come back to the quayside. Once the cargo was all unloaded the *Merchant Enterprise* was to go into dry dock for a few days before loading a new cargo. Dusty said that if all went well they would be back at sea within the week. For a whole day Wee Dick searched round the quay and the town for his friend Tinka. He found him in the late afternoon at the other side of the quay. If he had been avoiding Dick he did not show it. He smiled and laughed when they met and looked sad when Dick told him that he would soon be going away again. Dick managed to explain that the next day they would have a trip together. He did not tell Tinka where they were going.

He told his friends on board ship that he and Tinka were going for a picnic together and asked if he could have a little money but he did not tell them where he was going either. He just said it was because it would be the last time that they would be together.

Simon asked him where he would be going but he just said, 'Oh, to see the sights, here and there.'

Simon was wise and cunning.

'The wee barrel boy's up to something,' he told Dusty. 'He's not telling us everything.'

'You're right there,' answered Dusty. 'But he always seems to come out on top. There's something lucky about that young lad.'

Tinka was at the gate of the docks on time.

They walked through the streets together until they came to the edge of the town. Dick was a bit worried that when

44

Tinka saw the camels waiting to go to the temple he would refuse to go. He had presumed that the camels would be there as they had been before but today there was not one in sight. It was too hot to attempt to cross the desert on foot.

Dick looked round him, wondering what to do next.

Then he remembered how he had seen the train following almost the same route. It turned away towards the quarries but that was not far from the temple. He grabbed Tinka's hand and pulled him towards the railway station.

Tinka grasped the idea of a free ride on the train very quickly, and Dick realised that he had certainly done this before. They made their way towards the sidings and after dodging about to keep out of sight of the railway workers they soon scrambled into an empty truck heading towards the quarry.

The train puffed and rattled as it crossed the rising plain. Soon Dick could see the ruined walls over to his left. He signalled to Tinka and they carefully dropped off the slow moving train.

As they crossed the burning sand towards the ruins Tinka realised where they were going and his face lost its smile. He did, however, trudge moodily along beside Dick and followed him through the gap in the wall.

The place was deserted and silent. Even the singing insects that chattered all day seemed to be quiet. Wee Dick had got so used to the sound of these insects chattering night and day that the silence gave him a strange feeling that there was something wrong.

It was almost as if they had stopped chattering as Tinka and he had entered the temple and were now watching them to see what they were going to do there. Wee Dick shook his head to get rid of this idea. He turned and looked at Tinka.

Tinka was looking quite miserable but Wee Dick took him firmly by the arm and walked on towards the pool.

There was no sign of the crocodile in the green, foul smelling pool. They made their way round to the end where the low archway could just be seen. To make absolutely sure that the crocodile was not about, Dick threw a large stone into the water. He waited for a moment and threw another and then a third. With the third splash he saw the V-shaped ripple appear and move slowly down the pool to where the stones had sunk.

Tinka was clearly terrified at what was happening as Wee Dick grabbed him and pushed him down into the archway. Dick pushed and pulled him until they were well inside the tunnel. Here he did not have the courage to try to escape alone. They crawled and then walked along in silence until they reached the light shining down the shaft. Again Wee Dick could see the staircase going up into the darkness. This time it was easy. As Wee Dick stepped on the loose paving the stone wall rumbled open.

'Come on, Tinka.' He pulled him into the hall behind him. 'Look.'

He pointed triumphantly down the pillared hall to the statue, quite forgetting that he had wanted to try to find out how the wall had opened, until he heard it thud shut behind him. He turned quickly to feel the stonework with his hands, but could not find any kind of mechanism.

He turned back to look at Tinka.

He was cowering against the wall shaking with fear, his hands covering his eyes. Dick took hold of his arm and pulled him down the hall towards the blue light shining up through the narrow slit in the floor, Tinka struggled to break free and lay face down on the ground crying.

It was no use Wee Dick's saying, 'It's all right, Tinka. It's only a statue. There's nothing to be afraid of.'

The words were soothing but Tinka knew little English and was not to be comforted. Dick left him and went forward to look down the opening in the floor, but as before he had to draw back as some kind of gas or fumes made his eyes smart. He went behind the statue to check that the shaft was still there. This time, he thought, he would not need Bobbin to guide him back into the daylight. He returned to the front of the statue.

Now he had his witness. All he had to do was go back with Tinka to confirm his story. But something was wrong – Tinka was nowhere to be seen!

He looked all over, in and out, behind and between the pillars. He went round the whole hall several times. He called and called but got no answer. Tinka had not been in the mood for playing hide and seek so where on earth had he gone? Had he found out how to open the wall and gone back?

Well if Tinka could do it so could he.

Once again he went carefully over the wall looking and feeling for cracks. The wall was smooth and solid. The paving below was firm. It looked as if he would have to climb back out the shaft as before and go back to the ship alone. What would he do if he got back but Tinka did not? His story would be as incredible as ever. He did not know where Tinka lived. He might not see him again before the *Merchant Enterprise* sailed.

The hall was gradually growing darker. The light as it flickered became dimmer each time. He went back over to the light to see if he could find out why this was happening. He peered down the opening. His eyes were stinging and filled with tears as he peered down.

Suddenly he saw a movement below him. He lay on his front and leaned over the edge. He was sure there was someone down there.

'Tinka. Tinka. Is that you?'

He stretched forward as far as he could, trying to see clearly through his streaming eyes. Then all of a sudden he felt himself falling. His arms waved as he tried to stop himself as he slipped head first into the opening. For one frantic moment he thought, 'I'm going to be killed.'

He felt his head hit the floor and he was knocked unconscious.

Underground

When he came to, he was lying on his back and floating high above him was the blue mist through which flashed the light. He sat up, but his head throbbed so badly that he had to lie back again. He stared up at the blue clouds which soothed him and made him feel quite drowsy.

He had forgotten about Tinka.

After some time he felt able to sit up and look around. As his eyes became used to the dim light he could see that he was in a dome shaped room that had three tunnel like openings leading out of it. He stood up and looked above him, but could not see any way of climbing back up into the hall. There was nothing to suggest which tunnel he should take so he slowly went into the first one. The tunnel seemed to be cut through rock, as the walls were rough and uneven. Every few metres a larger lump of rock jutted out into the tunnel. These lumps seemed to glow with the same bluish light that he had seen before. Some lumps were brilliant while others hardly glowed at all.

His head still ached a bit so he did not think much about it but was glad that he could see where he was going. The path seemed to go steadily downward. He walked on until the tunnel came to an abrupt end at some roughly cut steps. These led down to a path running alongside water, rather like

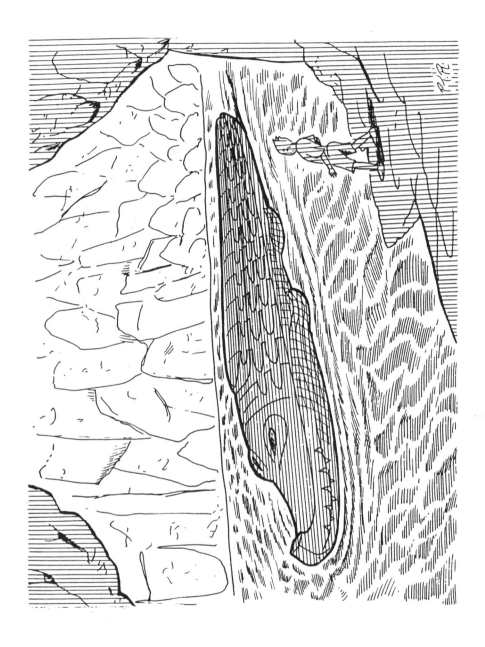

the canal towpath near his school. As he got closer he saw that the water was flowing rapidly into another dimly lit tunnel. He was on the bottom step when he noticed something moving against the current. He stepped back and flattened himself against the rock. He could look across the water and what he saw made his hair stand on end.

A crocodile, so huge it must have come from the age of prehistoric monsters! It was such a gigantic beast it could not have been the one from the pool. He watched in silence as it moved closer and closer. It was only as it neared the steps that he was able to see that it was not a real animal at all. It was a boat, a canal barge, decorated and disguised as a terrifying reptile, and indeed it had looked terrifying as it had come out of the dim light. As it slowly glided past he looked carefully, he could not see any windows or port holes, but he could see the water foaming gently behind where the propeller must be. The engine, if there was one, was absolutely silent.

He forgot his sore head. This was fantastic. He wanted to find out how to get aboard this strange boat and where it was going. When he got back to the *Merchant Enterprise*, this would be a story to tell.

He decided to walk along the pathway in case another boat came along. Perhaps he could attract the attention of some of the crew.

It was a dull uninteresting walk along the bank following the water as it curved and wound its way through the rock tunnel.

The tunnel became gradually wider until it opened out into a kind of cave. A crocodile boat was moored at a wooden landing stage. There were some stone bollards along the water's edge.

Except for the sound of the water lapping against the side

of the boat he could hear nothing. He stepped onto the gangway to look at the side of the boat more closely.

The outline of the door was quite clear, but it had no handle. He knocked, gently at first and then more loudly but there was no reply. He pressed his ear to the door but there was no sound from inside.

'Well,' he thought, 'someone must have tied up the boat so they must come back, but when?'

He walked a little farther along the path, past the boat and on into the tunnel again. It seemed to stretch straight ahead as far as he could see. He began to feel a bit dizzy so he turned back towards the boat. As he approached this time he could see that the door was now open.

'Is there anybody there?' he called in at the entrance. There was no reply, only an eerie feeling that there was in fact nobody there. He stepped cautiously on board and at once the door shut behind him with a firm sharp click.

He was on board a narrow craft in a small passageway with doors on either side. The first door he tried was locked but the second opened into a small cabin, a much smaller version of his own cabin on the *Merchant Enterprise.*

Suddenly he felt a slight movement, his dizziness seemed to be returning and then he realised that the boat was moving. He felt strange and put out his hand to steady himself.

Before he could reach the bunk, he passed out.

When he opened his eyes again he was lying on the bunk with a thin blanket wrapped around him. Someone had taken off his shoes. He lay still looking round him.

The cabin was small. Across from the bed was a door which was standing open and he could see into a tiny bathroom.

At the side of the bunk was a covered porthole. He put his

hand up to pull back the cover. He had to hold it tightly as it was on a strong spring ready to snap back into position as soon as he released his hold. He sat up and pulled it aside to peep out. The barge was moving steadily. Glowing blue rocks floating past the porthole told him that they were inside a tunnel and there was little else to see. The rocks floating past the window had a hypnotic effect and he began to feel drowsy so he lay back in the bunk and closed his eyes. He lay there thinking about all that had happened. It seemed a long time since he had left the *Merchant Enterprise* for this trip.

How long was it? Could it be days? Was it day or night outside? What were his friends doing? Nobby, Dusty, Simon, Tinka.

Tinka! Where was Tinka?

Just then the door opened silently and a man came in. He was dressed in some kind of uniform, a blue tunic over shorts and he wore a sort of veil covering his face. He carried a tray which he laid on the table beside the bunk, then turned and went out as swiftly and silently as he had come in.

'Wait!' called Wee Dick.

He jumped down from the bunk and flung himself at the door after the man but he was too late, the door was shut and locked again.

He turned back and looked at the tray. Only then he realised that he was hungry.

There was a plate of stew and some thickly cut crusty bread which was delicious. He ate some fruit and drank the pale pink fruit drink from the jug. There was little else to do once he had eaten, but he spent the next hours alternately looking out of the porthole and lying on his bunk watching a small red spider spin a web in the corner above his head.

He was looking out of the porthole when a slight click at

55

the door caught him unawares. He spun round just in time to see the tall man leaving the cabin. He had taken the tray away but left another jug of the pink fruity juice.

He tried the door but it had been locked again behind the man, and everything was quiet and still as before. He took another drink from the jug and went back to his porthole. This time there was a change.

The barge had moved out of the tunnel and was now in a large underground lake. This was lit by the blue rocks shining from the walls which were now a good distance away from the boat. The light was dim but he was able to make out the shape of another crocodile boat. This one seemed to have a headlight which was shining out over the water. The barges seemed to be heading towards a stone jetty. A third boat was tied up there, and he could make out people. As the boat moved closer to the jetty Wee Dick could make out buildings, which seemed to tower above him and touch the roof of the cave.

There was one very large building which looked much more important than the others. It was reached by a long flight of steps which led up to three tall arches. This building seemed to be built right into the rock itself and had no windows that Dick could see. He lost sight of it suddenly as his barge glided alongside the jetty. He watched the people there. They were all looking at his barge and seemed to be very excited. Two men in the tunic uniform moored the barge to bollards and the gangway was lowered.

There was a stir of excitement amongst the onlookers. Dick could not see what they were looking and pointing at. Then they began to make a loud hissing sound and moved back to allow something through.

The something was tied to a pole which was carried by two

men on their shoulders. As it passed the porthole, Wee Dick saw, to his horror, that the thing they were carrying, wrapped in a net and tied tightly to the pole, was Tinka.

His head hung back, just inches from the porthole, and in those few seconds he could not make out if Tinka was dead or alive.

The cover of the porthole snapped back as Dick released his hold. His legs were shaking and his heart pounding against his ribs. He felt hot and dizzy.

What did this mean? What had Tinka done? Was that going to happen to him too? How could he escape?

A few minutes later the door opened and one of the men came in. He made a movement with his hand to tell Dick to come with him. Dick sat there too afraid to move. The man waved again. What should he do? The man was big and strong. He got up slowly and followed him through the door, along the passage to the top of the gangway.

He walked shakily down on to the jetty but no hissing sound greeted him. The people smiled, they put their hands together as if praying and bowed their heads slightly as he passed. Two men went before him and two more followed behind. They went along the jetty until they came to the steps leading up to the three arches. At the top of the steps they were met by two other men who led him into the building. These men wore the same uniforms but without the face veils and they smiled and nodded at Wee Dick as they went upstairs and along corridors to a large room where they left him, locking the door behind them.

The room had very little furniture, a table, a couch and a cupboard which was completely empty. There were no windows. Blue Light streamed in through smooth panels on the walls. It was cold and silent.

Once he had wandered round the room Dick sat on the couch. He was not tired and was still very shaken by his brief glimpse of Tinka.

What was going to happen to him?

Some time later the door opened. A tall thin man came in. He had a short cloak that reached his elbows over his tunic, round his head he was wearing a thin band of yellow metal with the head of a crocodile forming the front of it. Dick thought that he looked to be the most important person he had seen so far.

He stood in front of Dick with his arms folded and looked at him for a few moments.

'You are English?'

'Well, no, actually I'm Scottish.'

'Ah yes, I know, that's the north part of England.'

'No, no. It's a separate country,' protested Wee Dick, but the man did not appear to be interested and carried on. 'You are welcome here. You will stay with us and be happy. Soon you will know us all.'

He spoke stiffly and carefully, as if he did not often speak English.

'Where am I? What is this place?'

Wee Dick wanted to ask a lot of questions, but either the man could not understand or he would not tell him what he wanted to know.

'I must get back to the ship. What day is this? We will be sailing soon and I must get back, can you take me back or show me where to go?'

No reply was given to any of these questions. The man just smiled, bowed and repeated, 'You will be happy here.'

This frightened Wee Dick who then asked about Tinka.

'Where is my friend?'

The man ignored him and moved to the door saying, 'Come with me.'

The corridor was busy with people, all moving in the same direction towards a large hall. The walls were of smooth stone and the ceiling above was the roof of the cave.

Some steps formed a low flat topped pyramid on which there were three stone chairs. Within a few moments the people stopped coming in. They talked to each other in whispers and soon even those died away. Most of the people were dressed in the tunic uniform. There did not seem to be many women there and no children at all. The blue light made it difficult to see anything really clearly. Everything looked dark and shadowy.

As he looked around anyone who caught his eye put his hands together, smiled and gave the slight bow.

Suddenly a gong sounded, echoing round the cave. The place became silent. Wee Dick's guide took him by the arm and led him to the foot of the pyramid. The gong sounded again. This seemed to be some sort of signal and everyone knelt. Dick found himself pushed to his knees by his companion. There was a movement at the back of the hall. He turned to see what was happening. All heads were bowed. Wee Dick bowed his but kept his eyes raised to watch what was going to happen.

A procession moved slowly down the middle of the hall.

It looked rather frightening, like crocodiles wearing long white gowns walking two by two. As they came nearer, he could see that they were men wearing hollow animal masks over their heads. When they reached the pyramid they parted and formed a row in front of it. The gong sounded for the third time.

Three men wearing long cloaks entered from the back of

60

the pyramid and sat on the chairs. Each wore a crocodile crown on his head. The two men on the outside chairs smiled and bowed but the man in the centre sat erect.

Dick could see that under his robe he wore ordinary clothes. He stared down at Dick and their eyes met.

It was then Dick realised that he was afraid. The man had a cold unsmiling face and looked at Dick as if he hated him.

'The Cold One,' thought Dick to himself as he bowed his head to avoid the cruel stare. The man on the right said something and the people stood again.

Two large strong men entered the cave carrying a long pole between them. From the middle of the pole hung a small cone shaped cage.

Tinka was hunched up inside. He looked half dead but his hands were clutching on to the sloping bars and his terrified eyes darted wildly round the hall. Even although he was a very small boy the cage was far too small for him. As the men approached the pyramid the hissing sound began again. Dick gasped, 'Tinka!'

The Cold One spoke in a strange sounding language that Dick could not understand. His words sounded harsh and cruel but the crowd nodded and made sounds of agreement. Tinka was then carried off through a small doorway at the side of the hall. The three men stood and went back down out of sight behind the pyramid. The procession turned and moved out. The meeting appeared to be over.

All round him the people nodded and smiled. Dick turned to his guide and said, 'That boy Tinka is my friend, why is he in a cage? Why did everyone hiss at him?'

'Don't let that concern you. You are our friend. He is not.'

'That's rubbish. He's just a boy like me.'

'Come, I will take you home.'

61

'Look, I haven't got time now. I'm not staying. I must get back to the ship. Tinka has got to come with me.'

'No, you will stay with us now. You will be happy here.'

'No, no, no! You don't understand. I can't stay. I must go. Now!'

The man just smiled at him.

Dick looked at him. There was no use trying to fight against him here. He would have to try to trick him.

'Well, I'll stay for a day or two. Can you let my friends on the ship know I'm all right?'

'Tell me more about your ship.'

'I'll tell you later,' answered Dick. 'You said you would show me your home, can I see it now?'

The man smiled. 'Our home,' he said.

They went back along the corridor to the three arches at the entrance. From here they could see across the other buildings to the underground lake stretching out into the mist of blue light.

'Just one thing before we start,' said Dick. His friend stood waiting, smiling. 'What is to happen to my friend Tinka?'

The man's smile vanished. 'Tinka will die,' he answered, staring out into the distance.

Escape

When Wee Dick heard this awful statement he was so horrified that he could say nothing. He could not even ask why such a terrible thing was going to happen. He knew that Tinka could not possibly have done anything so bad that he would have to die for it. There must be something very wrong with the people in this underground place. It did not matter that they smiled and nodded at him and said that he would be happy here. He would have to get out as quickly as he could, and he would have to find some way of getting Tinka out as well. He would make friends with this guide, or guard and learn as much as he could to help him plan his escape.

They went down into the lakeside town. The houses all seemed to be empty and looked as if no one had lived in them for some time. They came to some workshops where men were busy carving crocodile designs on panels of wood, cutting the same patterns round the rims of bowls and making small crocodile ornaments out of a soft white stone. By the jetty crocodile barges were being loaded from the buildings nearby which seemed to be warehouses.

Dick's guide spoke little and ignored most of Dick's questions like, 'Where did the people come from before they lived here?'

'Do they live in the cave all their lives?'

'How old is this place?'

'What makes the blue light?'

Either the man knew very little English or he was just not going to tell him. Perhaps he didn't trust him. Wherever they went the people smiled at Wee Dick and were proud and pleased to show him their work.

After about an hour they returned to the big building and Dick was taken back to the room with the couch. He saw that a meal had been left on the table for him. He ate it slowly and waited, hoping that perhaps someone would come to take away his dirty plates, but nobody appeared.

He wandered over to the door where he noticed a small flat plate beside the hinge. He stretched up to touch it and the door opened. He immediately closed it and tried again. The door opened again. He had discovered how it worked. So he was not a complete prisoner. He slipped out of the room and into the corridor, to wander around the building and look for a way out.

The rooms seemed to be built on three levels round the great hall. Most of them had arched entrances but no doors or windows. The light came from panels in the walls. Some of the empty rooms were in darkness. The people he saw were all working but stopped as he passed to nod and smile at him and hold out pieces of work for him to look at.

From the top level he was able to look down into the great hall.

He could see the pyramid and at the side the little doorway through which Tinka had been taken.

He went downstairs again to the hall and round to the door. Looking round to make sure that there was no one watching he pressed his hand on the plate at the hinge. The door opened quietly and Wee Dick slipped inside.

He found himself in a rough corridor cut out of the rock. It was dark as the lights were very faint, almost as if whatever made the rocks glow was dying. Small rooms went off either side of this corridor but none of them had doors and they were all very dark.

Feeling his way along, he followed the wall, which seemed to curve round, almost in a circle, thought Dick. He stopped when he heard voices and pulled himself back into the shadow close to the wall.

There were two men guarding an open archway through which Dick could just make out what looked like a spiral staircase. The men wore the tunic uniform and they both carried long spears which ended in sharp looking points. They were walking back and forwards in front of the arch. Could it be that Tinka was somewhere in there?

He thought for a few moments, then walked boldly forwards smiling to the men. They smiled and nodded back at him but as he tried to walk on through the arch they shook their heads and crossed their spears to bar his way. This made him positive that Tinka was somewhere inside. He was not going to be able to push through so he nodded at the men and walked off along the corridor.

Out of sight he stopped and thought for a few moments then turned and walked back again. He smiled as he passed the guards but deliberately did not look at the archway. He would come back again soon.

When he got back to his room he saw that the dirty plates were gone and some fresh fruit left. Soon afterwards his guide came back bringing him a light blanket. He seemed to be a little more willing to talk this time, so Wee Dick asked him how he would know whether it was night or day.

'The signal comes,' was the answer. 'There are three

signals: the first is for sunrise, the second is when it is time to eat and the third is for sunset.'

He did not have to wait long before he heard the signal which seemed to come from across the lake, a low moaning sound, but his guide would not explain any more. 'The sun has set,' he said, turned and left him.

Wee Dick had had a long day and was tired so he lay down on the couch and soon fell asleep. At first he slept well but then he had some very vivid dreams of crocodiles and cages and woke up with a start from his nightmare. He had no idea of the time until he heard the low moaning sound that seemed to be all around him telling him that it was morning. The sun had risen.

The day that followed felt endless. He explored the little town by the lake. The water on either side of the jetty looked dark and deep and the walls of the cave went straight down into the water. Near the wall of the cave at one side a great fall of stone had made a rough kind of beach. When the rocks fell they must have destroyed some buildings, for here and there ruined walls stuck up through the rocks.

What interested Dick most however were some small canoes and rowing boats tied by rope to a ring fastened to one of the walls. Perhaps he could use one of these to help him escape.

He returned to explore the big building again and made a second trip to the corridor to see if the guards were still there. Two different guards were on patrol across the archway but Wee Dick kept back, hidden from their sight.

He decided to go back again after the sunset signal had sounded. He was not sure just how much time he had to rescue Tinka.

He waited excitedly after the sunset signal until he thought everything was quiet, then he slipped out of his room. The corridor was empty and silent. He went first to the entrance and looked out over the town, it was quiet and still. To make sure of his escape he ran down to the shore and pulled one of the canoes on to the beach. Then he hurried back to the main building across the great hall and into the little corridor. Perhaps the guards would be away at night.

Dick knew this was not going to be easy.

Only one guard was on duty. He was walking back and forwards across the archway. Dick counted six steps this way, six steps back. The guard looked tired. Dick suddenly knew what he was going to do. He slipped off his shoes and stuffed one into each pocket.

Four, five, six, the guard turned.

He now had his back to Dick. This was the moment. He ran forward on his bare feet and slipped into the darkness of the inside of the arched opening, just as the guard turned again to make his return steps.

Dick crouched breathlessly behind the wall. He listened and counted the guard's steps. He was safe – for a time.

He looked around in the dim light. The spiral staircase he had seen from outside rose only a few steps and came to an end at the roof. He would have to go down. He began to tiptoe slowly down the stairs keeping close into the wall where it was dark. He did not notice however that as he moved one of his shoes fell out of his pocket and now lay on the first step where it could be clearly seen from the corridor. The stairs twisted round several times before he reached the foot where there was another smaller archway. This one was closed by an iron gate. The bars were close together. He looked through and there was Tinka in the cone shaped cage dangling from a large hook, only just clear of the floor.

The gate was held shut by a bar that slid through two slots and was locked by a pin on the outside. It opened easily.

Tinka did not notice him at first and he had to keep calling his name softly. Even then the boy was so tired and weak that he did not realise who was speaking to him. When he did his eyes filled with tears.

'Help me! Please help me!'

The first thing was to get him out of that cage. It hung only a hand's breadth from the floor but the hook was bent. By tugging and pulling at the chain and shaking the cage Wee Dick managed to get it off the hook but how did it open?

Dick looked around to see where he was. It was rather like being inside a hollow beehive. At one side of the room was a pool of dark water with some broad steps leading down into it. The room was well lit by the blue light and he could see quite clearly. From the shape of the cage he could see that it must have been placed over Tinka. The bars met at a point at the top and were far too strong for either or both of them to bend apart. The bottom of the cage must come off. As he examined the bottom of the cage he saw that Tinka's feet were cut and raw in places. He would not be able to walk either quickly or far.

He realised that the cage fitted into its base, rather like a light bulb into a socket. If he could just turn the cage a little Tinka would be free.

With an enormous effort he gripped two of the bars and pushed. The cage turned very slightly on its base and then sprang back into position as Dick relaxed his hold. He tried again but again the cage snapped back.

He rested for a moment and then with a deep breath he tried for the third time. Suddenly one of the bars sprang free leaving a space just wide enough for him to pull Tinka out onto the floor.

Tinka was almost too weak to stand. Dick propped him against the wall and gave him a drink of water from the pool. Then he gently pulled Tinka unsteadily to his feet.

'I'll try to carry you. For a bit anyway,' he said.

He hoisted Tinka on to his back. They had just reached the gate when there was the sound of voices. Someone was coming down the stairs. Wee Dick staggered under the weight of his burden into the shadow behind the foot of the spiral staircase. Two guards were coming down the stairs. One was carrying Dick's shoe.

As soon as they reached the gate they noticed the empty cage and with a shout ran forward to it.

Dick acted quickly. He slid Tinka off his shoulders and rushed back to the gate slamming it shut with a crash. He slid the iron bar back through the slots and put the pin into position to lock it. He might be able to gain some time. The men turned as they heard the crash in time to see Wee Dick pulling Tinka back on to his feet. They were just about to start up the stairs when a loud sound from inside the cell made them stop and look back. It came from the pool.

A large crocodile had come out of the pool and was moving across the floor with a speed that Wee Dick would never have thought possible of such a large clumsy looking animal. The huge reptile snapped at the guard nearest it who stepped back but the beast came on and its huge jaws closed on the man's leg. He gave a terrible scream as he fell.

Dick and Tinka were frozen to the spot as the crocodile dragged his prey round the cell. The man was still screaming as the crocodile dragged him down and into the water.

That sight Dick would remember all his life. It was all over in seconds – but there was worse to come.

The other guard shook frantically at the gate and tried to reach the locking pin. Forgetting that he had hoped to gain some time, Dick turned back to free the man. He had not reached the gate, however, when he saw that another crocodile was slowly prowling round the cell.

The guard saw him approach the gate but the beast was there too. He let go of the bars and edged away, backing round the small room against the wall, the beast increased his speed. The terrified man tried to move faster but slipped on the wet steps at the edge of the pool and fell backwards into the water. With a low growl the beast launched itself after him. There was a tremendous splash and the water foamed and bubbled. Then all was still.

It was over at last.

Wee Dick sat down on the bottom step feeling that he might be sick.

If anyone else had come down the stair he could not have moved. Tinka came and sat beside him and leant his head on his shoulder.

They sat there in silence for a few moments till Dick realised what was happening. Tinka must have been meant as food for the crocodiles. He shuddered.

If they did not move quickly they might both go back there.

He pulled Tinka to his feet and on up the stairs. The corridor was clear. The whole building was silent and empty. They did not stop again until they reached his room. Wee Dick knew that they could not stay there long. He had lost track of the time and it could not be long before the moaning horn would sound for sunrise. They ate some fruit and drank the rest of the fruit juice.

'Come on, Tinka. We can't stay here. We've got to go. Can you walk just a little farther?'

Tinka stood up slowly and hobbled painfully across the floor. It would be a slow journey.

Dick turned, hoisted his little friend onto his back and set off through the corridors to the entrance and down the steps.

They had just reached the foot of the steps when the sunrise horn sounded. Then he ran. Through the streets and down to the rocky shore. The canoe was where he had left it. He put Tinka into it and said, 'Stay here, I'm going to get some food from that warehouse. I won't be long.'

He ran back to the warehouse where he had seen baskets of fruit and bread. He grabbed some bread and a bunch of bananas and raced back to the shore. The streets were beginning to fill with people.

When he got back to the shore he stopped and stared – the canoe had been untied and was drifting out into the lake!

Wee Dick had forgotten just how little English Tinka understood. He must have thought he was to use the canoe to escape himself. The jetty was busy now that the men were back at work and Wee Dick could not risk calling out over the water. He just stood and watched the canoe drift into the distance. Tinka must be lying on the bottom and would not see him.

He had no other choice. It would not be long before the disappearance of the guards was discovered. Slowly he pulled another canoe ashore, watching around in case anyone should notice what he was doing.

When he was sure it was out of sight of the buildings he climbed in and pushed off from the rocks as hard as he could in the direction in which he had last seen Tinka's canoe. The mooring rope slipped into the water with a splash which to Dick sounded so loud that he half expected it to be followed by a shout as the men noticed what was happening. But

73

nothing happened.

He lay still in the bottom of the boat looking up at the dim shape of the cave roof until he thought it might be safe to peep over the edge.

He had drifted well out into the lake and the outline of the buildings was already faint. There was now no sign of Tinka's boat. He could see that the lake was not as large as he had thought because the rock walls on the other side were becoming clearer. He could already make out several cave like openings through which the water from the lake was pouring in fast flowing rivers. He was aware too that his little boat had been caught in a current and he was heading straight for one of these openings. He watched as it came nearer and nearer and he was swept into white frothing rapids. He clung tightly to the edge of the canoe as it was tossed along through this new tunnel. He was aware of a dull roaring sound which was growing louder and louder. Suddenly he realised what it was. He was being carried to the edge of a waterfall. There was nothing he could do to prevent his canoe from being carried over. He clung on tightly and shut his eyes. The canoe was swept forward until it balanced for one long moment on the edge and then tipped over. There was a wild roaring, Dick felt himself turning over and over but he clung on grimly.

A few seconds later he realised that he was floating again, he had survived the fall. He opened his eyes and looked over the edge. The canoe had righted itself and was floating in a shallow swirling stream.

He was not far from shore so he jumped into the water and waded ashore. He sat down on the bank to decide what he should do next. It was warm and his clothes soon dried, although he had lost his food.

Farther along the tunnel he could see a row of twinkling

lights, almost like a row of street lights showing him the way. Perhaps there would be a town where he could get something to eat. He set off in that direction. As he got nearer the lights he saw that they were in fact hanging baskets filled with glowing rocks. There must be people nearby, he thought. He was not sure that he wanted to see any one and he moved along close to the wall ready to hide if necessary.

At the end of the row of lights was a door. It looked a very ordinary door with a keyhole and a handle. Very cautiously Dick stretched out his hand and slowly pressed down the handle. The door opened quietly and inside was a long flight of stairs.

'I am always going up and down stairs here,' thought Wee Dick, as he trudged wearily to the top.

At the top was a brightly lit passage with several doors going off it. He listened carefully at each door before trying to open it. There was a store room full of boxes, a workroom with a bench on which were scattered parts of what looked like an engine, a bathroom and a kitchen with a large pot of something bubbling on the stove. This made him feel hungry again so he picked up a slice of bread and crammed it into his mouth.

He had just come out of the kitchen when he heard voices so he darted quickly into the next room and closed the door behind him.

He was in a bedroom, not like the room he had been given, but with furniture, like a bedroom in a hotel. He could hear a man's voice speaking in the strange language of these underground people but his accent was different, and although it sounded as if it was from another country there was something familiar about it.

The voices seemed to be coming from the kitchen. He

looked round the room wondering what to do next.

On the dressing table was a photograph of a girl, who might have been about his own age. He had not seen any children here at all and she really did not look as if she belonged in this place. She could easily have been a girl in his own class at school. School!

That reminded him he had to get back to the *Merchant Enterprise*, or had she already sailed for home? What would the crew have done about his disappearance?

A door shut and he heard footsteps in the corridor outside. They stopped at the bedroom door. Someone was coming in. He threw himself onto the floor and crawled under the bed. The door opened and Wee Dick could see a man's feet crossing the room. He stopped at the dressing table and then crossed back again to sit at a table. He seemed to be writing something. There was the sound of rustling papers. Then the man got up and came over to sit on the bed. Wee Dick could have touched his heels. He took off his shoes and wriggled his toes. Then he bent forward to take off his socks. For one long moment there was no movement. Then the man knelt down and looked under the bed.

His hand grabbed Wee Dick by an ankle and he was pulled out from his hiding place. He was lifted on to his feet and the man looked at him sternly. Wee Dick looked back. This was not a man from the caves. He was just like the sailors on the *Merchant Enterprise.*

'Well then, what have we got here?' he said in perfect English.

Malcolm and Fiona

'I'm safe! I'm safe!' gasped Wee Dick as he looked up at the man who was holding him by the shoulders.

'Not as long as you're here, little boy,' answered the man. 'You had better tell me all about it. And don't miss anything out.'

Wee Dick began his story, he told the man all about his trip on the *Merchant Enterprise*, meeting Tinka, the crocodile pool, his journey underground and finally the scene in the cell when he released Tinka. As he relived this hideous experience he got so upset that he started to cry and his whole body shook with his sobs. The man put his hand over his mouth and said, 'Shhhhhhhhh! They'll hear you! You're not out of trouble yet. But don't worry, I'll help you. What happened at the pool was not your fault. Your pal Tinka was meant to be crocodile food, you saved him. That's all right. You couldn't have known that the crocodiles were in there. Now listen carefully. My name is Malcolm and I can help you but I'll need a little time. Are you hungry? Wait here, I'll make sure that there's no one about.'

Malcolm went over to the door and looked out into the corridor.

'Come on now,' he said. 'They are all back at work, if you come into the kitchen we'll get you something to eat and then you will have to stay in here till it's dark.'

They went into the kitchen where Wee Dick washed his face and had a large bowl of warm soup and some bread and cheese. He felt much better but he was still worried about Tinka.

'There's a pretty good chance that your little friend has escaped,' said Malcolm. 'The lake is part of a dammed up river. It flows out through three channels. You went over the waterfall but the other two channels lead out through the rapids. If your little friend lay still in his canoe he'd shoot over the rapids and out into the open in no time. Then he would float down to the port and be free. You are not free yet but you have been very lucky. You do seem to be a lucky boy and you could be able to help me, but now it is time for you to have a rest.'

His meal had made him drowsy and it was not long before he was sound asleep. When he woke Malcolm was sitting by the bed watching him.

'It's night now. We must go quickly. They are all away till sunrise.'

'Why do they not sleep in the caves?' asked Dick.

'There are reasons,' answered Malcolm, 'but they don't concern you. It's just lucky for you that they don't stay here. Now I'm going to take you somewhere you will be safe until I can get you out of here. Then it will be up to you and your own good luck. But you seem to be a lucky boy, don't you?'

Wee Dick looked at him and smiled. 'Can I ask you questions?'

'Yes, but I don't promise to answer them,' replied Malcolm seriously.

The questions came tumbling out: Where is this place? What makes the blue light? Why were the men making things down here and what did they do with them? Why did some men wear crocodile masks? Who was the Cold One? Why was Tinka to be fed to the crocodiles?

Malcolm held up his hand.

'Steady on there,' he said. 'That's enough to be going on with. You want to know too much. Some things it is better for you not to know. The Cold One, that is a good name for him. He's the boss here, or would like to be. He and I don't always agree.'

'Why are you here, Malcolm?'

'Like you,' Malcolm answered, 'I am sort of on the run.'

'Does that mean you did something bad? Are the police after you? Did you kill somebody? Is there a gang after you?'

Malcolm laughed and said, 'I think you watch too much television, young man. The caves here are very old. A long, long time ago there were two different peoples living here. They had different customs and traditions. One race worshipped a god that was half man half crocodile. The others worshipped a god that they said had no face and could not be seen because he was so powerful. These peoples argued about their gods so much that they grew to hate each other and there were many battles and killings. A great war broke out between these peoples. It lasted for years. The final battle nearly destroyed both nations. The blue eyed people retreated and were chased into the caves. They had to cross a great swamp where many crocodiles lived but the floods came and they were trapped. The crocodiles fed as they had never fed before. There were few survivors. They never fought again but the hatred lived on. The blue eyed people said that their crocodile god had saved them and warned their enemies that if they came near the caves again they would be fed to the crocodiles. That was all a long, long time ago but children are still told the stories and dark eyed people never go near the caves. They believe that they are haunted.'

So part of the mystery had been explained, but not all.

'Anyway, there is no more time for stories now. We have got to go.'

They went along the corridor to the far end where there was a window overlooking a workshop where carpets were being woven. There was work on looms and rolls of carpet stacked on trollies ready to be taken away. They went down stairs and crossed this workshop into a dark cave at the edge of a swift flowing waterway, rolls of carpet were stacked along one wall.

'Look here,' said Malcolm. 'I'll show you the secret.'

He went over to a roll of dark green carpet and pulled at the end. It fell off like a lid. It was not a roll of carpet but a hollow tube covered by carpet.

'This is how I will smuggle you out, the day after tomorrow. This roll has had lots of uses over the past years, now it has a new use.'

'I'll suffocate in there,' objected Wee Dick.

'Oh no, you won't. I'll tell you more about it before you go.'

He led Wee Dick back along the passage, then into another one and then up some narrow steep steps that had been cut out of the rock, like inside the wall of an old castle. At the top was a small dark room.

'I've made it as comfortable as possible. It won't be for long. You should be safe in here. I'll come back when I can. Now remember, your only hope of getting away is by not being found. No matter how bored or curious you are, you must stay here. Do you understand? When I come you'll hear me whistle. Now make sure you keep hidden and quiet.'

81

Malcolm turned and left. The room became very still. Malcolm had left a torch so Dick shone it round to take a closer look at his new prison. There was a small mattress with some blankets and cushions against one wall, a folding camp stool, and a cardboard box with some bread, cheese, fruit and a large bottle of fruit juice. Dick did not like being alone here. It was rather like being built up in the walls of a castle. He had read about that happening to people in the Middle Ages.

Malcolm kept his word and visited him regularly. He brought him a large pullover and a pair of trainers. He told Dick that his shoe had been found near the crocodile pool and that the people thought that he had died there along with the guards and Tinka.

'So I would not like to be you if they find out that you are still alive,' he went on. 'We have to be very careful that they don't find out. Tomorrow will be your last day here, but this evening you will have a visitor.'

'Who is it?' asked Dick curiously. 'Who else knows I'm here? Is it Tinka?'

'No, it's not Tinka. You ask too many questions. At the moment the less you know, the better, just be patient and you will find out.' With that Malcolm turned and Dick was left alone again.

The day seemed endless with nothing to do. The battery in the torch grew weak. Dick was just about ready to fall asleep when he heard Malcolm's whistle but to his surprise it was a little girl that came into the cave carrying his meal on a tray.

'Hello Dick, I'm Fiona.'

She was about the same height as Dick and had long fair hair tied back in a pony tail. Dick looked at her. It was the girl that he had seen in the photograph in Malcolm's room. Her

English was clear but had a strange foreign accent as if she more often spoke the language of the cave people.

'I'm to stay here and keep you company until Malcolm gets back,' she said.

'Is Malcolm your father?' asked Dick.

'I have no father or mother,' she answered. 'Malcolm is my friend. He told me that you are going to take me back to my grandparents. Do you know them?'

'I don't know,' answered Dick. 'Where do they live? Who are they?'

'Malcolm will tell you all about it,' she said. 'I think they are very rich, Malcolm told me that they live in a big house.'

Malcolm returned early in the evening to tell them what was going to happen the next day.

'The carpets will be loaded on to the barges in the morning then the barges will sail down river and out of the caves to a trading post. There they will be transferred to a steam boat which will take them down river to the port. You will stay hidden inside the hollow carpet tube until you are on the steamboat. Once it sails you can come out. The captain is a friend and he will make sure that you get safely back to the seaport,' Malcolm explained.

'Then I will go and see my grandparents in their big house,' said Fiona. She was excited about the adventure she was about to begin.

She chattered excitedly about her grandparents until Malcolm said that she had to sleep for a while before they left. She went over to the mattress, lay down and before long she was asleep. Malcolm came and sat down on the floor beside Wee Dick.

'A few years ago there were two scientists working here,' he began. 'They had their baby girl with them. The man became ill and the family set off by boat down river to see the doctor at the seaport. As they were travelling downstream the floods from the mountains came and caught up with them. The river burst its banks and their little boat was carried into the swamps. The people here would not help in the search for them because they were afraid of the crocodiles living in the marshes so they were deserted. The boat drifted in the marshes, the man died and his wife caught a fever. She died shortly after I found them but the baby was all right. She has stayed here with me ever since. But she should go to her own people. I want you to take her home with you.'

'Why didn't you take her yourself?'

'I have business here, I must stay here,' Malcolm replied.

'Do her grandparents know that she is here?'

'No, but I have letters for you. You will take them with you and send them when you get safely back to your ship.'

'Why does she have to go now?'

'It is not a good place here for boys and girls. The glowing rocks could be dangerous. That's enough questions for now. It is time for you to get some sleep. I will wake you when it is time for us to leave.'

Dick lay on a blanket but felt restless. There were so many thoughts going round in his head about Malcolm and Fiona and the journey that they were going to make. However, after a while he did fall asleep.

Fiona was still sleeping when Malcolm woke him. 'It's time to go. Fiona will sleep for some time yet, I gave her something to make her sleep so that she would not make a noise.'

Malcolm carried Fiona and they set off through the corridors to the wharf.

The carpets were already loaded onto the barge.

'Right then, here's your hideout.' He pulled the lid off the carpeted tube. 'There's some food and fruit juice in this bag which should be enough.' Malcolm bent and slipped Fiona into the roll. He gave Dick a plastic wallet.

'Keep these safe. They are important letters for you to send when you reach safety. Now take care of yourselves and good luck.'

The sunrise horn began to moan. Dick crawled into the hollow tube behind Fiona and Malcolm put on the lid. He pulled a large tarpaulin over the carpets and left. Again Wee Dick was on his own. But not quite. This time there was a little girl that he had to help. Malcolm had given him a small torch so it was not completely dark. He shone it around. Fiona was still sleeping. He made his way to the top of the tube and carefully pulled the lid to the side. From here he could peep out. The tarpaulin was not completely down so he was able to watch what was going on outside. The barge was out in the open, he could see sunshine and blue sky above, which after his time underground was wonderful. He lay there watching the sky above him. Suddenly he became aware of a whimpering sound. Fiona was awake and was crying softly.

'I don't want to go. I want to go back to Malcolm. It's dark here. I don't like it.'

'He's coming later. There's nothing to cry about. I'll look after you,' soothed Wee Dick. Fiona was not to be comforted.

He was frightened that someone would hear her crying so he showed her how they could look out and see what was happening. They lay peeping out under the tarpaulin watching the channel grow wider.

There were plants and bushes growing along the banks and they could hear birds. Fiona became calmer and told Dick a little about her life.

She had never been to school but Malcolm had taught her how to read and write. She had never played with other children as there were none in the caves. She had visited the town once with Malcolm but that had been a long time ago and she could not remember much about it except that there were lots of ships there.

The barge moved slowly and as the day passed into evening the sky changed to dark blue and stars began to appear.

Perhaps because she had never been with other children Fiona had been rather spoiled, as evening wore on she began to get cross and moody. When they ate the food that Malcolm had given them she complained that she didn't like it. She said she was too hot, and that she wanted to go out and have a walk ashore.

'There are crocodiles out there,' said Dick. 'If you go out there they could eat you.'

'It's not fair,' moaned Fiona. 'Malcolm said you were to look after me and you are not looking after me properly, making me stay in this tube. I'm going out. I don't care if they do see me. I'll just ask them to take me back to Malcolm.'

'But what about me? If you do that they'll feed me to the crocodiles,' argued Wee Dick in desperation.

He wished more and more that he did not have to look after this girl.

She turned her back on him sulkily and said nothing more. A short time later Dick realised to his relief that she had fallen asleep.

He woke early in the morning. A mist was drifting across the water and the air was cold. When he peeped out he saw that they were moored by a wooden jetty among tall reeds. Now was the time that they were to wait quietly to be loaded onto the river steamer. He was glad that Fiona was still sleeping. She would not wait here patiently for much longer.

Suddenly he realised that there was something wrong.

There was the sound of yelling, shouting and loud banging noises like gunfire. The barge suddenly bumped against something so hard that he felt the carpets and his tube shift. He shook Fiona awake and dragged her out of the tube and pushed her under the tarpaulin. Their barge had broken loose from the others and was floating out into the river.

Tied up at the wharf the leading barge was on fire. Men were running about on the wharf but he could not make out what they were doing because of the thick black smoke rising from the burning barge.

There was a huge explosion.

Burning timber from the barge was thrown everywhere. It fell hissing into the water and onto the other barges. A small fire started on the tarpaulin on their own barge. Dick jumped up and stamped it out.

They were now out in the full flow of the river which was carrying them farther and farther away from the shore. They were alone on the barge at the mercy of the current. Fiona began to cry.

Wee Dick remembered that Malcolm had told them a steamboat was expected to collect the carpets. The captain would be sure to see them, he told Fiona reassuringly. They floated on through the morning but there was no sign of the boat. The land on either side became flat with no landmarks other than a few bushes and trees.

The barge developed a heavy list to one side and Dick and Fiona were startled when several rolls of carpet slid over the side.

They drifted into some shallower water among tall reeds.

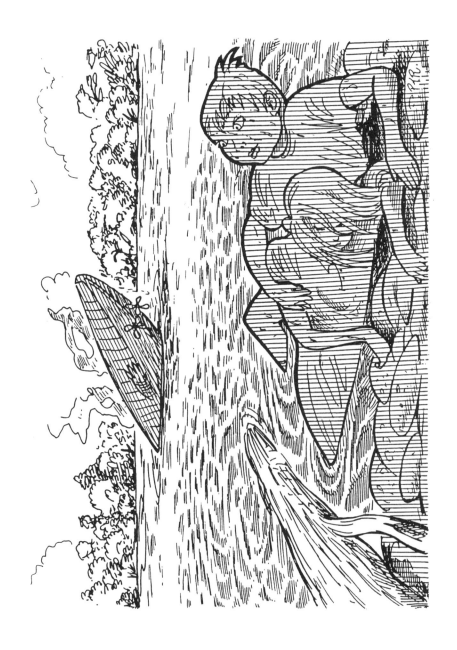

There was a crunching sound as they hit something under the water and stopped, jammed against a half submerged tree. Water came pouring in. Their boat was slowly sinking. Dick pulled Fiona to the edge and on to the trunk of the fallen tree that had blocked their way. They edged along the trunk to the shore and turned just in time to see their barge slip under water.

'We'll go this way,' said Dick, pointing downstream, still hoping that the steamboat might appear.

'That's no use,' replied Fiona. 'But look, there are people over that way. They could help us. We should go to them.'

'How do you know that?' asked Dick.

'Look,' answered Fiona, pointing to several bundles of branches lying beside the path. 'That has been gathered as firewood for cooking fires. We must be near a village, come on.'

They walked on for a few moments and then he could smell something, a mixture of woodsmoke, cooking and spices.

'Look. It's there in front of us,' said Fiona.

They crept nearer hiding behind the bushes as they went. Dick heard a strange bird like whistle close to his ear and turned round. There was a boy with dark curly hair and a wide grin standing behind him.

The Village

Dick looked at the boy, he had a sharp pointed face and ears, but dark laughing eyes. He was wearing a pair of ragged shorts and had a bright band of cloth tied round his dark curly hair.

Wee Dick felt as he looked at the boy's wide happy grin that he could trust him. He did not look like any of the people he had seen in the caves. He did not even look like Tinka.

Fiona spoke to him in the cave language. She had to speak very slowly and keep repeating herself before the boy seemed to understand.

'Does he understand you?' asked Wee Dick anxiously.

'Well, only a little,' she answered, 'but he speaks a different language.' She went on speaking to the boy, helping out her words with gestures and signals. Finally the boy spoke to her.

Dick could not understand anything and waited impatiently, kicking his feet in the warm sand.

'His name is Muza,' explained Fiona at last. 'He was whistling to warn his people that there are strangers about. They are all hiding. They think that people who come down the river from the mountains bring trouble.'

Muza whistled again like some exotic bird.

'That's to tell them that it's all right and they can come out again because we come from another country and are not

90

cave people.'

As they turned and walked towards the houses the villagers began to appear from behind trees and carried on with their own tasks.

The village was neat and tidy. The houses were made from a variety of materials, bamboo, wood, metal sheets and old doors. They were built round an open square where there were cooking fires and four large clay ovens. Women were busy working here, watching over the bubbling clay pots. The men seemed to be building a new house at the other side of the square. There were one or two old bicycles propped up against the walls of one of the larger buildings. The villagers were all quiet friendly people with the same pointed faces and ears and dark curly hair like Muza. There was one young man who knew a few English words.

'Hello, Goodbye and Thank you.'

He kept repeating them over and over again, laughing and grinning as he did so. Fiona found that some of the women understood her if she spoke slowly.

'They know that we do not come from the mountains, so they are not afraid of us,' she explained to Wee Dick. 'We can stay here and they will find someone to take us to the port. If we want to go on the river we will have to walk to the next village but we can wait and they will take us when they go to market. They don't use the river here because that always means trouble.'

When Fiona told them about the barge and the carpets there was great excitement. The news spread quickly. The men stopped work and gathered round the fires talking in anxious whispers. Then everyone set off for the river. The villagers headed straight for the spot where the barge lay half submerged, caught by the roots of the fallen tree. The last few carpets that had not rolled into the water were hauled off and thrown out into the river.

The men got busy with their tools and in no time the boat was taken to pieces. Nothing was left. The timber was carried back to the village where some was put on the fires and the rest hidden in the great woodpiles. The sand was raked over and not a trace of the barge remained.

Fiona told Dick that there had been a lot of trouble with men from the mountains, many of their people had been killed and the villagers did not want any more trouble because of the boat.

Muza took Dick and Fiona back to his home with his family that night. They shared a good meal and then Muza's mother brought in a bowl of a dark brown liquid. She spoke to Fiona who nodded and then explained, 'It's dye,' she said. 'They say it is not safe for us to be here. We have got to hide until they can get us away safely. We are to dress and look like them until we can go.'

Muza's mother combed the dark dye through their hair and cut Fiona's long hair very short. It made her look quite different. Dick was sure that no one would recognise her now. He was given a pair of brightly coloured, rather ragged shorts and a headband like Muza, Fiona was given a loose dress like the other girls. Muza's father took away their own clothes and Wee Dick watched rather afraid as he saw him burn them on one of the cooking fires.

The next day they were given work along with the boys and girls of the village. Fiona went with the women and worked preparing food in the kitchen area while Wee Dick went off with Muza.

It was late in the afternoon of the next day when the trouble began. Fiona and a group of girls were away collecting

firewood, Wee Dick and Muza were working with the boys making little round pots of red clay. The peace and quiet was suddenly disturbed by the sound of a car engine. It appeared bumping along the rough tracks between the bushes and stopped in the open square. The villagers looked up but carried on with their work. The boys working with Wee Dick crowded round to keep him hidden from the men in the car. A tall figure got out of the car and crossed the square.

Wee Dick could see that it was none other than the Cold One himself. He was wearing ordinary clothes but Wee Dick still felt afraid of him. He kept his head down and worked on his lump of clay. The Cold One walked around the village and spoke to some of the villagers. After a while he returned to the car but before he got in he gave a long piercing look round the village.

The engine started and the car turned. Wee Dick raised his head and watched it. The second man had never left the car. He had his back to him but Dick was sure that it was Malcolm. If it had not been for Muza and his friends he would have called out to him.

The car drove off. He felt puzzled and frightened. He did not tell Fiona what had happened but Muza's father told them that they would be leaving the next day because it was no longer safe for them to stay.

Muza's family were going to the next village to Muza's cousin's wedding. Dick and Fiona were to come too.

They set off early in the morning. Everyone came to see them off. Dick and Fiona were a little sad to say goodbye to the people who had been so kind to them.

They walked all morning until it became too hot to go any farther, then they rested in the shade and had a meal. It was early evening when they reached their destination. This village was much bigger than Muza's village. The inhabitants told them that they too had had a visit from the Cold One and his friend. They were looking for a boy and a girl they were told.

'You will have to take care. He is very dangerous.'

It seemed that the Cold One was not liked much here either. Wee Dick was puzzled by this information. Malcolm had told him that when his shoe was found he was believed to have been killed with the guards at the crocodile pool. He wondered what Malcolm had said when Fiona's disappearance was noticed.

But how did the Cold One know *he* was still alive? And why was Malcolm with him on the search to find them? He spoke to Fiona about it.

'Did you tell anyone that you were going away?' he asked.

She looked away and said nothing.

'Well did you?' he repeated, getting angry. Her eyes filled with tears. 'Tell me, it's important. I need to know.'

Finally she admitted that she had told her own special servant, Gohan. 'He was my only friend there other than Malcolm. He promised not to tell. He wanted to come with me and see the big house. I said that I would ask my grandparents if he could come too once I got there.'

'Didn't Malcolm warn you not to tell anybody?' gasped Wee Dick in amazement.

'I didn't tell ANY body. Gohan was special, he was my friend.'

'Well you may have got Malcolm into trouble,' said Wee Dick. 'There are people looking for us.' He did not tell her that he thought that one of the people was Malcolm himself.

Just then Muza arrived, grinning from ear to ear and looking very excited. He was a bright clever boy with a good memory and was proud that he was learning English. He had learned quite a lot while Wee Dick was struggling to master this new village language.

'News! News!' he cried. 'Your friend well. Him in boat down river.'

News of Tinka!

The people in this village had heard about the fight and fire at the jetty. They had heard that the mountain people had captured a boy from the enemy race and were going to sacrifice him to their crocodile god.

The boy had managed to escape in a canoe down the river and was found by his own people who were angry at the mountain people so had attacked their ships at the jetty as revenge.

So Tinka was safe. Dick felt glad of that and wondered if they would ever meet again.

Muza told him that all the villagers along the river bank lived in fear of the Cold One. There was often trouble but they would all be glad when someone escaped from the terrible mountain people.

Fiona said that the Cold One was a sort of king. Everyone was afraid of him except Malcolm, but he would never speak about him. He would often go away for weeks but no one knew where he went.

This village had a stone pier jutting out into the river but there were no boats at the water's edge. They were all moored well back among the reeds and covered with branches to hide them. Dick looked at them and thought to himself that it would not be too difficult to push one out into the river and then travel downstream to the port. It was a plan that he would have to think about.

Muza pointed down stream. 'Look!' he cried.

The steamboat was slowly coming up river.

She sounded her horn and everyone ran to the jetty. She was a small broad vessel called the *Princess Royal*. She had a tall old fashioned funnel, a mast and an open bridge with a canvas awning covering the deck. The people on board were laughing, singing and waving. More guests were arriving for the wedding. They came ashore to join the happy crowd making its way up to the square.

Dick and Fiona turned to join them and as they did so they froze. There, leaning on the rail watching the crowd stood the Cold One with no trace of a smile on his hard cruel face. Dick pulled Fiona into the crowd.

The wedding celebrations were about to begin. The girls formed chains of dancers and wound their way round the village, more joining the chain as it passed each house. The boys made their own chain in a separate dance with much shouting and stamping. Wee Dick and Fiona joined in all the excitement. As it began to grow dark more fires were lit and strange musical instruments appeared. Two straw huts were built, one at each end of a long table. The music, laughing and dancing continued late into the night.

Dick could not remember when he finally went to sleep that night but almost as soon as it was dawn the celebrations began again. Fiona was dressed like the other girls in special wedding clothes. Dick did not recognise her until she spoke. Her disguise was perfect. She had a brightly coloured dress and wore golden bangles and long earrings shaped like flowers. She had a head-dress of golden leaves from which was fixed a dark veil which completely covered her. Her eyebrows had been painted black and her face made up to look like the rest of the village girls.

Dick was dressed up too. He was given a pair of wide baggy trousers and a short brightly coloured cape. For his

98

head he was given a kind of helmet shaped like a bird with feathers on the top and a long tail that hung down his back.

Dick had never been at a wedding. He watched all that was going on, fascinated. The music began and the groom entered the circle and sat in one of the straw huts.

Then the girls led in the bride. Dick had never seen anyone wearing so much gold. Gold thread in her dress glittered in the sunlight. She wore bracelets, rings, earrings and a thin gold veil covered her from head to foot. The wedding ceremony seemed simple. The bride sat in the other straw hut. The groom got up and crossed over to take a golden band off his head and put it onto the bride's. Then the two huts were set on fire. This was the signal for a great cheer and the music, singing and dancing began again. There was a great feast and plenty to drink.

Muza handed him a cup of a green coloured liquid with a nod and a smile. It looked like lime juice but it made him cough as he swallowed.

Dick joined in all the fun and games, the singing and the dancing. He remembered at one time seeing the Cold One sitting on a chair outside one of the huts watching all that was going on with his steady unsmiling eyes. Now when he looked the chair was empty.

He was having fun. Fiona was dancing with the other girls, Dick turned and again joined the chain of boys stamping and dancing round the fire. The dancing grew faster and faster. Suddenly he lost his grip and staggered away from the chain.

He tripped over the roots of a tree and fell, hitting his head on the trunk. When he sat up his head was spinning.

The bright glittering crowd of dancing people swayed and

swirled before him. The sky above him was dark blue with thousands and thousands of stars. Beautiful stars.

Beautiful stars.

Towards Freedom

It was the middle of the morning when Wee Dick woke up. He was still lying under the tree and was stiff and sore. He stretched himself and looked around. The whole village was silent. He got up and wandered across to the village centre. It was empty now. The fires were now piles of grey ash, and some birds flew up from the tables where they had been enjoying the remains of the wedding feast. He wandered down to the water's edge and discovered that the *Princess Royal* had sailed during the night. He and Fiona had lost that chance of escape.

Soon the sleeping village began to wake.

The crew of the *Princess Royal* ran down to the jetty but their ship had gone with only the engineer and a fireman on board. The worried sailors shouted angrily and waved their hands but Wee Dick could not understand their language.

Fiona and Muza had disappeared during the night.

The anxious villagers searched every hut, but there was no trace of either of them. No one seemed to know where they had last been seen.

Wee Dick felt very alone. He could not understand what the people were saying and he could not ask questions to help him know what was happening. He wandered around the village feeling miserable.

He gathered that the villagers were going to set off to the next village down river to get help and that they would take him with them when they were ready to go. The villagers all got busy clearing up the remains of the party and packing food for their journey downstream.

Wee Dick stood at the water's edge. There were some small covered boats here. He looked at them. He knew that he had to find someone who spoke English to help him. He had to get down river to the port as quickly as possible. If he could launch one of these boats the current would take it on its way. But these were heavier boats than the little canoes. He would never be able to launch one of these on his own.

There was one very close to the water's edge. He went over to it and pushed it but it didn't move. He began to rock it back and forward from side to side. It made a slight movement. Encouraged he rocked harder but as he did so it tilted right over. A man's body rolled out of the boat so unexpectedly that Wee Dick jumped back in fright. The man lay on his back, so still that at first Wee Dick thought he was dead. Then he heard a low moaning. The man was wearing the tunic uniform of the mountain people, his face was covered with blood.

Wee Dick turned and ran back to find Muza's father. He pulled his arm, dragging him towards the shore. The villagers followed and the wounded man was soon brought back to the village where he was washed and given clean clothes.

He was badly hurt, with two nasty looking wounds. The villagers made signs to Dick to tell him that these were bullet wounds.

The man was able to speak a little. Dick could not understand what he said but as he spoke he saw his friends' faces grow anxious. Whatever he said hastened the departure from the village.

They followed a narrow track well off the dusty road and kept moving even through the hottest part of the day. Towards late afternoon they could see the houses of the next village. The farther downstream the villages were the bigger they became. This one had several stone and brick built houses.

They went into the village in small groups. Wee Dick stayed with Muza's father and two uncles. The place seemed to be deserted. As they walked round the houses the only sound that could be heard was the hum of the singing insects. In front of one of the large houses Dick saw the car – the car that the Cold One had used when he had visited Muza's village!

It was a wreck. The windscreen and windows were smashed, the tyres were flat, the doors were bashed and a dark pool of oil was growing under it.

It was early evening and shadows were growing as they walked towards the quay. There was a large warehouse here. As they passed it Dick noticed a piece of veil caught in the door. It was just like the one that Fiona had been wearing the night before. He pointed it out to Muza's father and they went on up the steps.

The door at the top was not locked and they went on into the dark warehouse. Here they found Muza. He was tied up and lying on the floor. The ropes that held him were very tight and his wrists and ankles were badly hurt.

There was great excitement amongst the villagers when Muza was found. They gathered round him all talking at once.

He was very weak and tired and was not able to say much. Wee Dick could not understand a word that was being said. He became frantic and walked up and down trying to work things out for himself. He noticed a door at the far end of the warehouse. Perhaps Fiona was tied up here too.

He went over to the door and looked into the small room behind. This was a small office. There were plans and charts pinned on the walls. An upturned chair was lying behind the desk under the window. He walked over to the window to look out.

On the sill were brown smears that looked like blood. Dick shivered. He looked out of the window. It was not too high up. He noticed that the plants that grew underneath it had been flattened, as if someone had been on top of them.

Only two metres away there was a small boat lying on the shore, just out of the water and no more. He could manage that one easily, he thought. It would not be stealing because he could return it once he had got help.

He climbed out onto the sill and dropped himself onto the soft plants below. He ran over to the boat and quickly pushed it into the water. Once he was on the water he let the little boat glide along bumping against the bank until the current pulled it into the mainstream of the river. The sun set as he began his journey. He had not thought about having to travel in the dark but it was too late now.

The boat had a small paddle at the stern. It was held by a metal ring so that it would not come loose and the boat could be steered by working the paddle. He had seen men in boats like this working round the harbour when he was on the *Merchant Enterprise*. Now he had to try it for himself.

He could see the lights on shore growing smaller. The river carried him along quickly. The steering paddle seemed to have little effect. The night was cool and there was a slight breeze. There were lights twinkling in the distance ahead of him. At first he thought they were stars but as his little craft was carried closer he realised that he was looking at the lights of a fairly large town. He didn't need to steer as the current carried him toward the shore. There were all sorts of boats moored to buoys. His boat bumped into one after another, spinning him round after each bump. There were two men in a small motor boat, Dick called out to them.

They came after him, and caught hold of his boat. They attached a rope to it and towed him along behind them to the quay.

Tied up at the quay was the *Princess Royal*, and leaning against the rail watching him being helped ashore was the Cold One himself.

Standing beside him showing no sign of fear what so ever was Fiona! Dick was given no choice. He was led up the gangway on to the *Princess Royal*.

'Dick, we've got to go back,' said Fiona. 'Malcolm's had an accident. He's broken his leg and he's been asking for me. That's why they've been looking for us.'

The Cold One watched Dick and Fiona without speaking.

Wee Dick was not convinced that this story was true but he was too afraid to say anything. The Cold One nodded and the two men who had brought him ashore hurried him below deck and locked him in a small cabin. There was a tiny porthole through which Dick could see the lights on shore but otherwise the cabin was in darkness. The ship was silent, not even the sound of voices. He was tired, hungry and thirsty, tears came to his eyes. He lay on the bunk and gradually drifted off to sleep.

He was wakened by the noise of the ship's engines and felt the vibration as it set off. He looked out of the port hole and saw the lights of the town slipping out of sight as the ship curved away from the quay. It was heading back up river.

He heard voices and footsteps, then a flickering light lit his cabin. It was inside a glass bowl set into the dividing wall between his cabin and the next so that one bulb lit the two cabins. Just then his door was unlocked.

One of the men from the motor boat led him along the passage to a small room where the Cold One and Fiona were sitting at a table. He was shown to a seat. Fiona looked as if she would like to talk. She kept her head down, but peeped up at Dick from time to time. She looked as if she had been crying. A bowl of a thick soup with some lumps of tough meat was served and then some fruit. They all ate in silence.

As Wee Dick was taken back to his cabin he noticed the other man from the motor boat come out of the cabin next to his. He carried a tray which he laid on the floor for a moment as he turned to lock the door. So, there was another prisoner on board.

Dick sat on his bunk and thought. Every turn of the propeller was taking him back to the mountains and the caves. He remembered Malcolm saying, 'I would not like to be you if they find out . . .'

The generator on the *Princess Royal* could not be very good. The lamp kept flickering and fading. Dick watched it and suddenly it gave him an idea.

Could it be Malcolm on the other side of the wall?

If he could take off that glass bowl he might be able to talk to whoever was on the other side. He climbed up on the stool and looked at the lamp. All he had to do was unscrew two small bolts. They were not tight and came away easily in his hand. The bowl slipped off easily and he peered past the flickering bulb into the next cabin. All he could see was the opposite wall. The bunk must be underneath the light.

106

'Malcolm, Malcolm. Are you in there?' he whispered. 'It's Dick. Can you hear me? Can you speak?'

To his delight a voice answered. It was Malcolm, his voice sounded tired but he could talk.

He told Dick that he had a bullet wound in his left foot which badly needed attention and he should see a doctor. He was a prisoner on the boat. There were some men from the caves as crew, and the fireman and engineer who were being forced to work at gunpoint. The *Princess Royal* was needing fuel and would not manage to go far up stream against the current until she had loaded more wood for her boilers. She would probably tie up at the next landing.

Malcolm asked Dick about Fiona.

When he heard she was on board too he said, 'Now listen, Dick. The Cold One, as you call him, does not speak English. You must tell Fiona I am here. Then we must make some plans to escape.'

It was a long night. The cabins were hot and stuffy. Malcolm was in pain and groaned in his sleep. Dick lay awake wondering what was going to happen next.

Next morning at breakfast Dick spoke to Fiona. 'Good morning, Fiona,' he said. 'We are prisoners on this ship and so is Malcolm. He is in the cabin next to mine. For goodness sake don't let HIM know what we're talking about.'

Fiona looked as if she had not slept well and her eyes were red from crying.

'Good morning, Dick,' she answered. 'Did you sleep well? Is he hurt?'

'Yes, his foot. He needs a doctor. You have got to help us. When the ship stops for wood you must find someone to help us.'

The Cold One spoke to Fiona sharply in his own language.

107

She put her head down and the rest of the meal was eaten in silence.

It was mid morning when the *Princess Royal* was steered clumsily alongside a quay. The porthole did not look out on the bank so Dick could not see where he was and there was no way that he could attract attention. Fiona, however, found herself alone. The Cold One had gone ashore and the other men were busy loading wood. She found it quite easy to lift the keys from their hook, go below and unlock the cabins.

Once they were together in Malcolm's cabin Dick and Fiona were able to see how badly injured Malcolm was. His foot was wrapped in badly bloodstained cloths. He had not shaved for several days and looked pale and ill. How would they be able to escape? Malcolm was obviously far too weak to walk for any distance.

Wee Dick decided to explore the ship to see if he could find any escape route. The cabins were at the front, the engine and boiler room in the middle and the hold where the wood was being loaded was at the stern. To get to the hold Dick would have to cross the engine room. Here the engineer and fireman were sitting on the floor being guarded by a man with a rifle.

Dick dropped to his knees. Very quietly he crept forward. Keeping behind the engine he made his way behind the guard towards the hold. If he could get ashore he might be able to get help.

Luck was with him. The guard did not turn round and Dick reached the hold. Two of the men from the village were loading. They signalled to Dick to keep quiet. He watched as they hid among the logs at the back of the hold and realised with relief that there were friends aboard. He crept quietly back to Malcolm's cabin to tell the news.

Malcolm and Fiona listened.

'And they can't lock you in again,' said Fiona triumphantly. 'I've thrown the keys into the water.'

'Well now, we have to wait and see what happens,' said Malcolm. 'But I think we should try to get out of here.'

It was a slow business, moving from the cabin. Malcolm was in a lot of pain and had to rest often. Dick kept a few paces ahead making sure that there was no one about as they made their way slowly back towards the engine room.

When Dick got there the guard was still on duty. When he turned round, however, Dick saw that the guard had changed. Now it was one of the friendlier villagers who stood holding the rifle. The fireman and engineer were still working but nodded and waved to Dick that it was safe to come on. Malcolm could go no farther. He lay down behind a large wooden chest. Dick and Fiona crouched close beside him.

It was early in the evening when the boat approached the wooden jetty where Dick had begun his escape down river. It was deserted and parts of it were badly burned. As the *Princess Royal* was brought in clumsily her bow struck the charred timber which collapsed into the water. She reversed back and her stern crunched against the jetty. One of the crew jumped ashore to tie her up.

There were loud yells from all around. Men seemed to rise up from the ground and there was uproar on board. Villagers appeared from hiding places all over the ship and from among the wood in the hold. There was yelling, shouting and the sound of gunfire. There was the sound of running feet on deck, thuds and crashes. Then things grew quieter, the battle seemed to have moved off the ship and onto the shore.

Wee Dick crept up on deck and peered around. The *Princess Royal* had been moored by only one rope at the stern and the

110

current had swung her round so that she was pointing out into the river.

It was growing dark and the fighting continued around the jetty. In the dim light it was difficult to make out who was friend or foe. There were screams and more shots were fired. The fight seemed to be moving away from the water front into the darkness. Then almost as if it had been switched off, the sound stopped.

There was silence.

Wee Dick could see what looked like a body on the jetty, it did not move and no one came to help. He went back down to tell Malcolm and Fiona what he had seen.

'We've got to get going, as soon as it's light. We've got to get back down river,' said Malcolm.

'But how?' asked Wee Dick, looking around him. 'By ourselves?'

The engineer and fireman had vanished as soon as the fighting began.

'Who else is there?'

'But what if they come back before morning?'

'Help me on deck,' said Malcolm. 'I know about ships like this. Just do what you are told and you will be all right.'

Between them Dick and Fiona supported Malcolm as he clung onto the handrail and hoisted himself up step by step. The ship was now about four metres from the quay.

'Nobody can come aboard without being seen,' he said. 'Now fetch me the rifle that guard dropped down there. We can keep watch.'

Malcolm's instructions were short and clear. Fiona was sent to bring a box of cartridges from the Cold One's cabin, then Dick and Fiona stoked the boiler with wood from the hold.

'Now bring me a blanket from a cabin,' ordered Malcolm. 'I'll keep watch from here and if I shout be ready to do exactly what I tell you.'

Malcolm examined the gauges in the engine room. 'We've got to be ready to move very quickly,' he said.

'But who's going to steer?' asked Wee Dick.

'You, my little sailor boy. Fiona will help me work the engine and the current will help.'

The warm night passed slowly into dawn and mist drifted over the land. There was a slight chill in the air and everything was very still.

'As soon as the fog lifts we're off.'

But the mist lingered. More and more wood was dragged from the hold and fed into the furnace. The sun was beginning to rise.

A faint noise was heard in the distance, gradually growing louder, it was the sound of motor boat engines. Suddenly the engines were switched off and silently, gliding out of the haze came three crocodile boats.

'Quick, cut the rope, Dick!' shouted Malcolm and handed him a long sharp looking knife.

At the stern Dick hacked at the rope which broke at his third cut. The *Princess Royal*, already pointing downstream, was caught by the current.

'I'm starting up the engine now,' shouted Malcolm. 'Get up there on the bridge and try to steer her straight. Remember, port's left, starboard's right.'

Dick knew nothing about steering ships but he had watched the captain of the *Merchant Enterprise*. He ran to the wheel, released it as Malcolm had shown him the night before and shouted, 'I'm ready.' He could hear the propeller turning.

'Starboard,' yelled Malcolm.

Dick pulled the wheel hard and the ship swung round towards the opposite bank of the river, and was in danger of running into the bank if Malcolm had not shouted, 'Port. Port. Hard to port.'

She had a start on the crocodile boats but with the mist gone they were in hot pursuit, their engines roaring.

Wee Dick hung onto the wheel and did his best to follow Malcolm's shouted directions. Two of the motor boats were drawing level with them.

Malcolm had dragged himself onto the bridge beside Dick. He had the rifle.

'Hard to port,' he yelled, but Wee Dick got confused and turned starboard.

The *Princess Royal* answered so promptly to the pull on the wheel that the motorboat could not pull away fast enough. There was a dragging scraping noise from the starboard side then the sound of shouting and men splashing in the water. Malcolm took the wheel.

'Look,' he said, pointing behind where the crocodile boat, its bow smashed, was sinking. The crocodile disguise was torn loose and was floating in the water. It was nothing but a thin plastic shell over a powerful motor boat.

The other boats left their sinking friends to themselves and chased on after the *Princess Royal.*

Malcolm gave the wheel back to Dick and took up the rifle. He fired at the boat on the port side. This made it slow a little but not for long. The powerful motor boats were faster than the old steam boat but they were steering well clear of another collision.

The boat on the port side slipped out from its crocodile cover as Dick watched and he saw the Cold One standing on deck, aiming a rifle at the bridge of the *Princess Royal.*

113

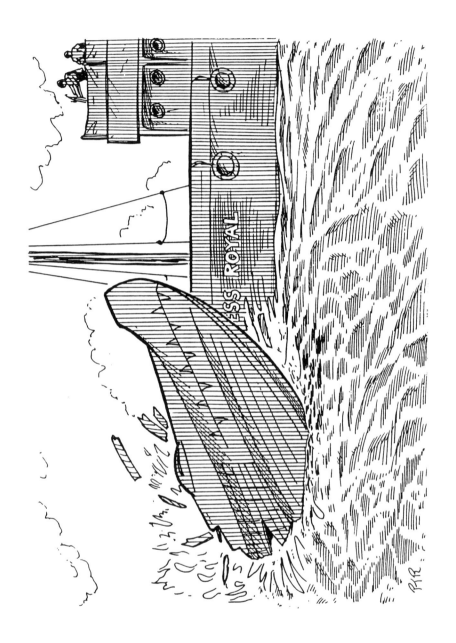

Whether his target was Wee Dick or Malcolm he missed both. The bullet hit the rail splitting it into long splinters.

In his fright Wee Dick did not start when Malcolm fired back. He did not see the Cold One jerk as the bullet hit him but he saw his body plunge into the river. Malcolm fired again, reloaded, and sent two more shots into the boat, as it slowed down to pick up the man in the water. He was being carried downstream and the motor boat was turning to catch him. Now black smoke was coming from the engine.

'Here, hold this,' said Malcolm and handed Dick the rifle.

He grabbed the wheel and swung the *Princess Royal* round in a wide circle to face back upstream, towards the smoking boat.

They had their own troubles on board and when they saw the *Princess Royal* bearing down on them, their attempts to change course were too late.

They did not have a chance. The steamboat struck them in the middle.

When Wee Dick looked back all he could see were some pieces of wood swirling in the ship's wake. He never saw the Cold One again.

All this time Fiona was in the engine room. Malcolm told Wee Dick to try to steer straight in midstream while he went below to make sure she was all right. Both the engine and the boiler were needing his attention, her speed had dropped so low that she was more or less being carried along by the current. Wee Dick was too late to notice that the *Princess Royal* was too close to the right bank.

After the collision, Malcolm had swung her to port, heading downstream again. This had brought her close to the shore. Wee Dick was too slow to be able to correct this and the ship slid along the muddy cliff snapping the roots and overhanging branches of trees until she rammed her bow into the soft earth.

The third motor boat had now lost its crocodile disguise. It had hung back after the second boat had been sunk but now that the steamship was grounded it came in closer. It headed towards the stern but did not come too close.

There seemed to be four men aboard. Malcolm fired at them but they cruised around at a safe distance then turned and sailed back up river, the sound of its engines growing fainter and fading away.

Malcolm decided to set the ship full speed astern. Wee Dick was to stay on the bridge and hold her straight. The first attempt to free her failed but the second try pulled her off the soft sand bank and back into the free flowing water. She was still moving backwards when Wee Dick looked over his shoulder and saw the motor boat. Her engine was silent and she was being carried close to them by the current.

'Look out, Malcolm. They're back!' he yelled.

The motor engine started up again and as the *Princess Royal* started to move forward, Wee Dick saw a man on the motor boat stand up and throw something on board. It was a bottle with a burning cloth stopper. It flew overhead and into the hold. Wee Dick shouted to Malcolm as a second bottle landed on deck but the flame had been blown out in its flight. The first bottle had however landed in the wood. It had got caught in a tangle of branches and was burning upright like a candle on a Christmas tree.

'Two can play tricks,' said Malcolm. 'Steer back towards the shore.'

As the ship ground and shuddered along the bank he told Wee Dick to come below.

'Now you two have to hide here no matter what happens.

They'll come back to see what's gone wrong and when they do, I've got a surprise for them.'

He took an iron bucket and filled it with some oil soaked rags and some broken sticks of firewood. He wedged the bucket into the tangle of branches and set it on fire. A convincing pillar of dark smoke and flames rose up out of the hold.

'Now, you two. Down behind that chest and stay there.'

Wee Dick and Fiona did as they were told.

They could hear the engine of the motor boat, cruising closer. The engine stopped very close to them. Dick saw Malcolm hurl the bottle with its lighted rag fuse back into the motor boat. There was the sound of smashing glass and a rifle shot. Something scraped along the side of the ship and then the engine room was lit by the flames of the burning motor boat. Wee Dick turned to see a man trying to climb aboard the *Princess Royal* but Malcolm pushed him in the chest with the butt of his rifle and he slipped back down into the water.

Malcolm hopped back over to the engine controls and with a shudder the engine started and the *Princess Royal* pulled out into the river.

Their troubles were not over, however. The burning bucket had toppled over and the firewood in the hold was now alight.

'Quick, get the extinguisher!' shouted Malcolm.

Wee Dick sprayed the contents of the extinguisher over the burning wood and Fiona ran round the ship to bring him another two. The fire out, they looked round to see that the motor boat had been abandoned and the remaining crew were struggling towards the riverbank. They watched them scramble up the soft earthy cliff just as the motor boat blew up, sending pieces of burning wood everywhere. Some of these landed on

117

the deck and Dick and Fiona ran to throw them overboard.

They were in a mess, they were dirty from the smoke and soot, only then did they feel the blisters on their fingers. Malcolm was exhausted, his foot was bleeding again and he was close to collapse. They helped him back to the engine room where he fell into a feverish sleep.

The *Princess Royal* sailed on slowly through the afternoon. Dick had got the hang of steering her and the current helped them along. By evening the wood had burned out and the engines stopped. Malcolm was unconscious, they could not rouse him. The river had widened a lot and they could see lights ahead but they were so far away that shouting seemed to be pointless.

Safety

It was almost dark when they saw the headlight of a power boat heading towards them. A powerful searchlight was switched on and they were boarded by sailors. Wee Dick was not familiar with their uniform. Some of the sailors spoke a little English, and explained that they were to be taken into the harbour. A tow line was attached to the *Princess Royal* and two sailors came on board to help steer. Malcolm was carried up on deck and the three of them were transferred to the launch for the journey into the harbour. During the journey a sailor cleaned Malcolm's foot and dressed it with clean bandages.

It was night but soon the lights of a big town came into sight. Here the electric lights showed that a crowd had gathered to watch them come ashore.

Malcolm was carried down the gangway on a stretcher and taken away in a car to the hospital, one of the sailors told Dick and Fiona. Dick and Fiona were taken to a house where a stout grey haired gentleman who spoke very good English was waiting for them. Here they had baths and were given some clean clothes and a good meal, before being shown to their bedrooms for the night. After the cabins on the boats Wee Dick could not believe that he could stay in such luxurious surroundings.

After breakfast the next morning the gentleman asked them to tell their story. He listened quietly. Now and again he would ask a question but mostly he listened quietly, nodding and saying, 'Go on, what happened next?'

Fiona asked about Malcolm.

'He is to stay in the hospital for a few days,' the gentleman told her. 'He may have to have an operation on his foot. Perhaps you could visit him in a few days time.'

They spent the afternoon playing in the swimming pool at the back of the house. The grey haired gentleman's wife made a great fuss over the two of them and brought them ice cream and fruit. After the evening meal their host took them back to the quay. The *Princess Royal* was now tied up there and her crew were busy cleaning and painting her.

Wee Dick and Fiona were taken to the power launch. They were to go on down the river to the main port. Their hosts and a crowd of people waved them off. Wee Dick and Fiona waved until they could not see the people any more and the launch turned a bend in the river, hiding the lights. Then they went into the small forward cabin where they soon fell asleep.

The bright sun streaming through the cabin window woke Wee Dick early the next morning and he went outside. The river here was wide and there were high buildings on either side. There were all kinds of boats moving about and over beside the cranes some large ships were unloading their cargoes.

As the launch came gliding in towards the jetty Dick saw what he had never expected to see again.

The *Merchant Enterprise* was moored there and towered high above him at the quayside.

'Look, Fiona! Look! Look!' he shouted. 'It's the *Merchant*

120

Enterprise. There's Dusty and I think that's Simon.'

He shouted and waved but his voice would not carry the distance above the noise of the quayside. He was sure that all he needed to do was to get ashore and go over to the ship and he was safe. But he and Fiona were taken from the launch to a big office building and up to the top in a lift, to a room with big windows that looked out over the river. Here they were questioned by three gentlemen who asked them to tell the story of their adventure over and over again.

It was then that Dick remembered the letters that Malcolm had given him. He did not have them and could not remember when he had last seen them. Fiona said that she had some letters but that they were in the drawer in her cabin on the *Princess Royal*. One of the gentlemen at the desk picked up a phone and gave some orders about having the cabins searched. A short while later the telephone rang and Fiona was told that there were no letters in the cabin.

They asked about Malcolm.

'He is in the hospital,' they were told. 'You will see him when he is well enough.'

At last they were free to go and walked out of the building and across to the *Merchant Enterprise*.

All work stopped there and the crew came to meet him at the gangway.

'What did I tell you?' Simon reminded his mates. 'The wee barrel boy always comes out on top.'

The wee barrel boy did not know where to go first. He pulled Fiona from one place to another, introducing her to all the sailors.

They were told that Fiona would be allowed to visit but she must stay at the house of one of the port officials. Wee Dick was disappointed. He thought that it would have been all

121

right for her to sail home with them in the *Merchant Enterprise* and find her grandparents.

The captain himself spoke to him about it.

'We cannot take her with us. It is quite impossible. No one here knows anything about her.'

The sailors told him that when he had disappeared from the *Merchant Enterprise* there was a search all over the port. The repairs had taken longer than expected so when Dick did not turn up after a few days they had sailed for their second port of call. There his monkey Bobbin had been left in the zoo. Now they had come on to this port where they were to stay for three more days before sailing for home. When it was time for Fiona to go ashore, a big stout man called Captain Pinnoah came for her.

He was one of the men who had asked all the questions about their adventure. He was dressed in a white uniform with a lot of gold braid and buttons. Wee Dick was not sure whether he was a sailor, or in the police or the army, but he carried a sword in a scabbard. Wee Dick never saw him without it. He had a wide happy smile and laughed a lot when he spoke to Dick and Fiona. As he led Fiona down the gangway he told Wee Dick that he would come back for him the next morning and take him on a trip.

He returned early the next morning, without Fiona. He told Wee Dick that Fiona had gone with some friends to see Malcolm. He did not say where, but Wee Dick never saw her again.

'Now my young man,' said Captain Pinnoah. 'We are going back up river in the patrol boat and you will show me all the places where you had your adventure.'

Dick was reluctant to go back up this river and seeing the frightened look on his face Captain Pinnoah added, 'You don't need to worry, you'll be quite safe. The patrol boat is big and fast and we will have you back here on your ship before it sails tomorrow.'

It was just as the captain had said, the patrol boat was a large cruiser with cabins on board. Wee Dick was thrilled by the speed as she set off upstream.

The journey passed quickly. During lunch the captain asked Wee Dick more questions about Malcolm's story of the scientists and their baby girl.

'We have never heard of people like that. It is difficult to believe that people would bring a young baby to work with them in the country. If, as you say, Fiona is nine, people would still remember her parents. We do not have a lot of strangers working in our country. We would not forget them.'

After lunch the captain said that they would visit the villages where all the things had happened. 'Then,' he said, 'we will question the people.'

Wee Dick thought that this would be easy, but although they stopped at several villages they all looked very much like each other. The villagers came to the jetties and laughed and smiled as they were questioned but he could not recognise any one. Of course nobody said that they had seen him before.

Captain Pinnoah kept laughing and smiling and indeed treated it all as if it were a huge joke.

'Better luck next time,' he would say, grinning at Wee Dick.

In the flat countryside there were no land marks for Wee Dick to remember, until late afternoon when he saw the wooden quay with its half burned timbers.

'There, there!' he cried in triumph. 'Look.'

'That place hasn't been used for years,' laughed Captain

Pinnoah. 'There was a fire there a long time ago.'

'It's no use going on,' cried Wee Dick. 'You don't believe me. You don't believe me one little bit.'

Captain Pinnoah did not answer him.

'Now we will go and search for your great caves,' he said.

The river was getting narrower and the mountains seemed to be closing in on them. The river was passing through a gorge. The scenery began to look more like that he had seen on his first trip. As the ship rounded a great curve Wee Dick could hear a loud roaring noise, almost like thunder that did not stop.

'What's that noise?' he asked.

'Don't you know? Well you shall see any moment now.'

The walls of the gorge seemed to open out like two gigantic doors. Ahead of them the river was coming down, in a waterfall so high that it seemed to come out of the sky itself. The noise made speech impossible. Spray rose from the falling water sending up a cloud of white mist. It was a wonderful beautiful sight.

The patrol boat circled in the waves below the falls. Then Captain Pinnoah gave the order to go back to port. Wee Dick was miserable. He had never seen this fall before.

The barge in which he and Fiona had left the caves could never have come this way. He didn't know what to do or say.

As the boat journeyed back, Captain Pinnoah pointed out an old stone quay beyond which a narrow track wound back into the mountains.

'Look there. That is where the mountain people come to load their goods and send them to the city.'

Dick knew that there was more to it than that but he also knew that there was something wrong. There was too much power against him. He knew that he had not dreamed his

124

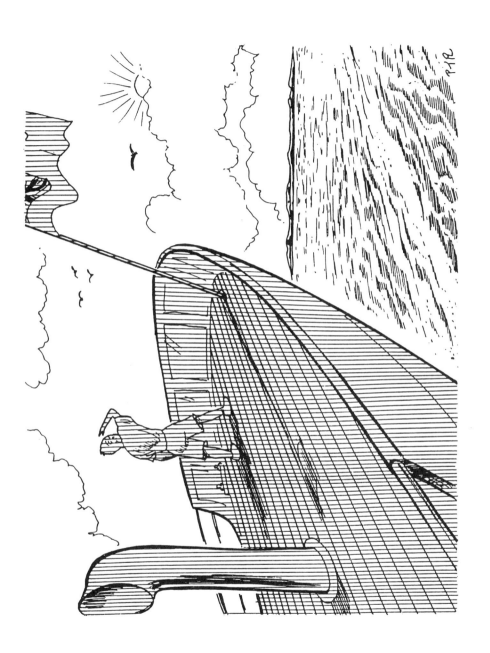

125

adventure.

Somewhere there was another stream that flowed into this one. One day he would find out. But for now he said nothing.

It was dark when they reached the port. The *Merchant Enterprise* was ready to sail. Simon was waiting for him and together they went to Dick's cabin.

There he told Simon all about the trip.

'They want me to think that I dreamed it all,' he said. 'But how could I? Why do they want it that way? I could not find any of the places where I'd been because they did not take me there. That's why.'

'Yes, lad. The people here are like that. They are not like us. It's just good that you are out of it safe and well. Tomorrow we'll be far away from here and you will soon forget all about it.' He said goodnight and left him.

One thing however Wee Dick was sure of, and that was he was NOT going to forget all about it.

It was Dusty who shook him awake in the morning. 'We're leaving in a few minutes. Come up on deck and say goodbye to your adventure land.'

Wee Dick stepped on deck and watched the city with its wharves and tall buildings slowly slip past the rail. The buildings gradually growing smaller as the ship got underway and the hills rising higher behind them. The river widened out into the estuary. Soon he was looking back from the open sea and could only make out a long purple outline of land on the horizon.

The *Merchant Enterprise* dipped and rolled on the waves. He was on his way home. He had left it all behind: Malcolm, Fiona, Muza, Tinka and his monkey Bobbin. One day he would come back to find out all the things that had not been explained to him properly.

Life on board ship was not the same as before, the sailors didn't seem so friendly. One afternoon when he was sitting in the shade with his special pals Dusty, Nobby and Simon he took out his fortune knot and the tiny wooden barrel.

'Well,' said Nobby. 'When are you going to pull the ropes apart and learn your fortune?'

'I'm not going to. I'm going to keep it as it is and give it to someone else,' answered Wee Dick, turning it over in his hands.

'So you'll be a fortune teller as well as a story teller,' they teased him.

Wee Dick shook his head and went off to another part of the ship on his own.

'What do you make of him?' asked Dusty.

'He tells stories,' said Nobby, 'and you're never sure where he gets them from. There's something strange about him all right. Look at him going missing in one port and then turning up in another with more stories.'

Simon had the last word, 'I think he went where he was not meant to go. He saw things that others wanted to be kept secret. Why should grown men like Captain Pinnoah bother about a wee laddie's stories and take so much trouble to make them out to be nonsense unless there was a lot of truth in them? There's something going on in those mountains. I wouldn't trust that Captain Pinnoah farther than I could throw him. When you get a lot of strange goings on like that, you can bet your life that there's money behind it somewhere.'

The weather grew colder and it was a grey misty day as the *Merchant Enterprise* began her journey back up river to her home port.

Wee Dick was anxious to see home again. He leant over the side peering through the mist, trying to get his first glimpse. Through the fog he could faintly make out his mother and father standing on the quayside. He put up his hand to wave but the mist thickened and swirled; he could not see whether they waved back or not.

'Dick! Dick!' he heard his mother's voice calling.

'Mum! Mum!' he tried to shout but his voice was drowned by the deep drumming of the engines.

The mist swirled around him, whiter and whiter, thicker and thicker. He couldn't see anything in front of him. He felt the deck shudder and shake under his feet and tried to take hold of the rail to stop himself from falling.

'It's all right. He's back again now,' he heard a voice beside him and turned to see who had spoken. Dimly through the mist he saw his mother and father again.

Their faces became clearer but everything was white around them. He looked round and saw that he was lying in a bed in a small room. The walls were white, the ceiling was white, and the sheets on the bed were white. At the foot of the bed stood his mother and father with a tall man in a white coat.

'He'll be all right now. I'll leave you together for a few minutes,' said the tall man who turned and left the room.

'Where am I? Where are Dusty and Simon?' asked Wee Dick.

His mother came over and stroked his head.

'It's all right, Dick. You are in hospital. You've had an accident. You've been unconscious for three days but you are going to be all right.'

'How did I get off the ship?' asked Wee Dick. He felt dizzy and a bit confused.

'The helicopter brought you here. You've been a very lucky little boy,' answered his father.

'Dad, I was in the caves with Tinka and I got lost. The men

129

were eaten by the crocodiles but Malcolm helped Fiona and me to escape. Nobody believes me.'

His father smiled at him and said, 'It'll be all right, son, in a few days.'

Just then the door opened and the tall man in the white coat returned.

'Well, I think that's enough for today. It's time for you to rest, young man, and I hope you won't try going to sea in a barrel again. It's just lucky you were picked up. You nearly drowned, you know.'

Wee Dick lay quietly, trying to take in what was being said.

'Thank you, Doctor,' said his mother. 'We'll leave him now and come back again later.'

His parents left and Wee Dick lay in bed trying to work out what had happened to him.

A short while later a nurse came in carrying a tray.

'Come on then. Sit up and try to eat something. That will make you feel better. If you can eat the sausage and chips there's some ice cream after.'

She laid the tray on the small table beside the bed. Dick sat up and turned to look at his meal.

Lying beside the tray, on the table were his fortune knot and the tiny wooden barrel.

'Now I KNOW it was real,' he said aloud as he fingered the knot gently.

Then he laid it back on the table beside the barrel, picked up the cutlery and began to eat his meal.